THE RISE OF FALSE MESSIAHS

The Rise of
False Messiahs

LEFT BEHIND
>THE KIDS<

Jerry B. Jenkins

Tim LaHaye

WITH CHRIS FABRY

TYNDALE HOUSE PUBLISHERS, INC.
WHEATON, ILLINOIS

Visit Tyndale's exciting Web site at www.tyndale.com

Discover the latest Left Behind news at www.leftbehind.com

Published in association with the literary agency of Alive Communications, Inc., 7680 Goddard Street, Suite 200, Colorado Springs, CO 80920.

Edited by Lorie Popp

ISBN 0-8423-5805-6, mass paper

Printed in the United States of America

08 07 06 05 04
8   7   6   5   4   3   2   1

To the Marshalls—
Jordan, Brent, Logan, Mikayla,
Jim, and Reba

TABLE OF CONTENTS

The Young Tribulation Force

Original members—Vicki Byrne, Judd Thompson, Lionel Washington

Other members—Mark, Conrad, Darrion, Janie, Charlie, Shelly, Melinda

Southern contingent—Carl, Tom, Luke

Other Believers

Chang Wong—Chinese teenager working in New Babylon

Tsion Ben-Judah—Jewish scholar who writes about prophecy

Colin and Becky Dial—Wisconsin couple

Sam Goldberg—Jewish teenager, Lionel's good friend

Mr. Mitchell Stein—Jewish friend of the Young Trib Force

Naomi Tiberius—computer whiz living in Petra

Chaim Rosenzweig—famous Israeli scientist

Tanya Spivey—daughter of Mountain Militia leader, Cyrus Spivey

Cheryl Tifanne—pregnant young lady from Iowa

Zeke Zuckermandel—disguise specialist for the Tribulation Force

Marshall Jameson—leader of the Avery, Wisconsin, believers

UNBELIEVERS

Nicolae Carpathia—leader of the Global Community

Leon Fortunato—Carpathia's right-hand man

What's Gone On Before

JUDD Thompson Jr. and the rest of the Young Tribulation Force are living the adventure of a lifetime. Judd and Lionel Washington travel to Petra and hear miraculous stories of God's power from Sam Goldberg and Mr. Stein.

Vicki Byrne and the others at Colin Dial's home are warned to leave the area. They hurry to the new hideout in Avery, Wisconsin, narrowly eluding Global Community forces. Vicki is glad to be back with the others but still worries about Judd.

With the help of Chang Wong in New Babylon and Chloe Williams in San Diego, Judd and Lionel find a Co-op flight to South Carolina and hurry to meet believers, Luke and Tom Gowin. Judd and Lionel notice two men with strange weapons walking along a trail. While escaping from their notice, Judd and Lionel discover Tom Gowin handcuffed in the back of a pickup truck. After a long chase, the bounty hunters catch Judd, Lionel, and Tom.

Join the Young Trib Force as they struggle to reunite with each other and survive the Great Tribulation.

ONE

Heading for
the Blade

JUDD Thompson Jr. said a quick prayer and wondered if it would be his last. He glanced at Tom Gowin, the young believer from South Carolina who lay on the dusty floor, his head turned, a trickle of blood running from his mouth.

Lionel Washington was beside Judd, his hands also cuffed behind him. Lionel was near tears, his head down, sweat pouring from his forehead.

Judd wondered where they had made their mistake. Were they wrong to come to South Carolina? Chang Wong kept up with developments around the world. Surely he knew the danger they faced.

"Keep your head up," Judd whispered to Lionel.

Someone slapped Judd on the back of the

head. "Shut up!" Albert yelled, pushing Judd hard. "Get in the next room."

The bounty hunters herded Judd and Lionel into the living room of the tiny house and shoved them onto a shabby couch by the front door. The man with the long scar on his face, Max, took out a cigarette and lit it. Judd noticed Nicks littering the kitchen table, payment for bringing in two bodies without the mark of Carpathia.

Max threw a leather pouch at Albert. "Put the money in there. We don't want anybody wiping us out while we're gone."

"You know there's nobody out here—," Albert began.

"Just do it," Max said, opening the door.

"Where you going?"

"The truck needs fuel." He glanced at Judd and Lionel. "And make sure the other one's still alive. If he isn't, we'll load them all up and take them to the GC."

The door slammed behind Max, and the truck chugged to a small outbuilding. Judd watched through a side window as Max unlocked a creaky door. Empty metal cans crashed until the man found one with gasoline.

Albert grabbed Nicks from the table and floor and stuffed them into the pouch. He jammed a few bills into his pockets, and

Judd gave Lionel a look. Albert smiled as he flitted about the room gathering money, humming an off-key version of a country song.

"We're going to do a little celebratin' tonight! After we turn you in and find that other nest of Judah-ites, we'll have enough money to move out of here and get a place near the city where the real money is."

Judd bit his lip. The pain from being shot by the weird weapon and having his hands cuffed tightly behind him had dulled his senses. It was difficult to breathe, let alone think clearly. His shoulder muscles ached as he shifted on the rickety couch.

"Too bad you and your friend are settling for chicken feed," Lionel said.

"Shut up," Albert said.

"Up in Atlanta, there's probably thousands of people without the mark. We could lead you to them."

The man grinned. "You ain't from Atlanta. I can tell you're from up north somewhere."

"I didn't know it mattered where we're from," Lionel said. "Isn't an unmarked Northerner worth just as much?"

Albert rolled his eyes. "Max says the GC is real interested in you two. They might pay us more than the regular rate."

3

Lionel glanced at Judd and leaned toward him, then whispered, "You think Tom's still alive? His head hit pretty hard on the floor."

Judd shrugged and the truck started up again, a plume of blue smoke rising from the tailpipe. Max pulled up to the house and ran inside. Albert handed him the bulging pouch of money.

"He kept some of it," Judd said.

Albert backhanded Judd's face. Judd tasted blood in his mouth.

"Judah-ites," Albert sneered. "He's just trying to get us to turn against each other."

"Look in his pockets," Judd said.

Another hard blow, a kick this time, sent Judd reeling. The couch crackled, and if Lionel hadn't been sitting beside him, Judd was sure they would have toppled.

"He took some of the money!" Judd yelled.

Max glared at his partner. "It had better all be here."

"I might have picked up a few Nicks by mistake . . ."

Max frowned at Albert who held out his hand. "I swear it was a mistake." He dug into his pockets, emptying the contents on the table.

Max grabbed the Nicks and shoved them

into the pouch. "I'm going to count this. If it's short—"

"Lemme look," Albert said, fishing in his pockets.

Judd saw movement to his right. Someone peered through the crack in the door where Tom was being held. Judd studied the face—a young man, a little older than Judd. Brown hair. *Luke?*

The man made a signal Judd couldn't understand, then mouthed, "Stay there."

Judd nodded and whispered to Lionel. When Judd glanced back, the door was closed.

The veins in Max's neck were sticking out. "Check on the other kid and make sure he's alive."

"Wait," Judd said, trying to stand.

"You shut up," Albert said, kicking Judd in the stomach and sending him back onto the couch. Judd tried to stall the man, but he went straight for the door. He jiggled the handle several times. "How did this get locked?"

Max squinted. "Out of the way!"

With one kick, the door cracked and flew open. Max and Albert disappeared into the room, and both let out a string of curses.

"The window!" Albert yelled. "He got out through the window!"

Vicki Byrne closed her eyes and tried to calm herself. The e-mail from Chang Wong in New Babylon was the worst news she could imagine. Bounty hunters in the South were looking for anyone without the mark of Carpathia. Judd and Lionel had walked into a trap.

Mark turned the speakerphone on so everyone could hear Carl Meninger's voice. Carl had worked for the Global Community in Florida and now lived in South Carolina.

"Tom and Luke headed for the fort hours ago," Carl said. "That's where they were supposed to meet Judd and Lionel."

"Have you had any contact with Tom and Luke?" Vicki said.

"We talked by radio several times. They saw Judd and Lionel's plane and even spotted them rowing across the river. They were going to meet them when we lost contact. I thought they had just gone out of range, but maybe they were caught."

"How far from the meeting place are you right now?" Mark said.

"It's a hike. We're a long way up the river on an old plantation."

"Those bounty hunters could be coming to you next," Vicki said.

"We don't see many people up here," Carl said. "We've taken a lot of precautions since our other hideout was discovered."

Carl said he would check back when he heard any news, and Mark hung up. An eerie silence fell over the group.

Finally, Zeke said, "I think we ought to pray."

The kids prayed for Judd, Lionel, Tom, and Luke. Vicki wiped away tears. A few minutes into the session, she got up and went outside.

Zeke joined her under one of the awnings the group had constructed between cabins. "I know you're upset, but you can't give up hope."

"I have to do something. The GC is making all the moves. It's like we're trapped."

"You know how long it would take you to get to South Carolina from here? The best thing you can do is pray."

"I don't want to pray. I want to do something!" Vicki sobbed.

Zeke nodded, his long hair swishing against his chubby shoulders. "I know exactly how you feel. When the GC picked up my dad, I wanted to go in there with guns blazing and get him out. You know how hard it is to know someone you love's going to die?"

Vicki couldn't speak.

Zeke put a hand on her shoulder. "Dad was ready, and Judd and Lionel are too."

"Don't talk like that! Judd's coming back, and I'm going to help him!"

Vicki ran inside the building. "I'm sorry to interrupt, but I need a vehicle."

Marshall Jameson stood. "Vicki, you can't be serious."

"I have to help them."

Shelly hugged Vicki and they both cried.

Mark ran a hand through his hair. "Vicki, this is insane."

She turned to Zeke. "Isn't there a part of you that wishes you had tried to save your dad? Don't you ever wonder if you might have been able to help him?"

Zeke just stared at her.

Colin Dial stepped forward. "If this program that Commander Fulcire created goes through, there'll be a million eyes watching. If everyone knows they can make money finding people without the mark of Carpathia, we'll be a prime target."

"The program hasn't started up here," Vicki said. "Besides, I'll stick to back roads—"

Becky Dial put a hand on Vicki's shoulder. "I know how upset you are, but Colin's right.

You can't go anywhere right now. We have to trust God."

"He helped you by sending that angel Anak," Charlie said. "Maybe God will send an angel to Judd."

Vicki looked from face to face, sensing their concern. Everyone in the room wanted Judd and Lionel to return safely.

"I'm going to my cabin," Vicki said. "Call me the moment you hear anything."

Vicki raced away, wiping tears from her face. She collapsed on her bunk and sobbed, crying out to God.

※

Judd caught his breath as the two men in the next room shoved wicker furniture away from the window. Lionel struggled to his feet and moved toward the kitchen.

"What are you doing?" Judd said.

Lionel turned and felt along the tabletop. His eyes lit and he scampered back to the couch. With his hands still cuffed behind him, he held out his pocketknife. "He took this and some clips from me earlier." He sat on the couch, leaning forward, trying to open the small blade.

Max returned and Lionel sat back, hiding the knife in his palm.

"Get these two into the back of the truck," Max said, glaring at Judd and Lionel. "And switch your gun to kill. No more trying to be nice to these kids."

Albert hustled Lionel and Judd into the back of the truck and closed the tailgate. Max had fastened plywood over the broken window, and it was dark inside.

"You try to get away and it'll be the last time," Albert said.

The plastic cuffs were tight around Judd's wrist, and Lionel said he had lost most of the feeling in his hands. Lionel told Judd to scoot close. He pricked Judd's arm once with the blade, and Judd helped guide the knife to the plastic strip.

Lionel pulled the blade back and forth along the plastic. With the sawing motion they hoped to cut a notch into the thick plastic.

"Good thing they didn't have the metal cuffs or there would be no way we'd get them off," Lionel said. "You think the guy you saw was Luke?"

"I've never seen him before, but I can't imagine who else it would be."

Judd held still as Lionel worked. Max and Albert hadn't returned, and Judd wondered if they had followed Tom into the woods. After a few minutes, Lionel pulled the knife away, and Judd managed to get his little finger to the middle of the cuffs.

"I don't feel any notch at all," Judd said. "It's not working."

"I have another blade with a serrated edge. Let me try that."

Judd helped guide the blade again, but this time the edge cut his arm and he yelped.

"Sorry, man," Lionel said.

Minutes later the bounty hunters returned, and Judd heard the clatter of a weapon in the front seat.

"You know I don't do well at that place," Albert whined.

"It's not like there's a bunch of gators down there," Max said. "Just take these two and have them processed. I'll stay here and wait on the dogs so we can find the other one."

"Max, let me stay."

Max spoke through clenched teeth. "Go. I'll find the other one."

The door closed and the truck started. Lionel kept working on the cuffs as they bounced along the bumpy road.

"You ever think it would end this way?" Lionel said. "Guess you won't get to see Vicki again."

"Concentrate!"

Judd didn't want to think about anything but getting free. Now, as Albert drove along the deeply rutted road, Judd thought of Vicki. Unless Tom got back to his group and told the story, no one would know about Judd's and Lionel's fate. *Is this God's plan?* Judd thought. *How could this possibly glorify God?*

Years before, Bruce Barnes had said, "Pray as if everything depends on God, but work as if everything depends on you."

Lionel stopped for a moment and worked out a cramp in his hand. "Feel it and see if we're making any progress."

Judd ran a little finger around the plastic, feeling for a notch. Lionel had been working the new blade long enough to get a cramp, but Judd's heart sank when the surface was completely smooth.

TWO

The Shoot-out

JUDD leaned forward and tried to relax. He had been straining to help Lionel cut the plastic bands since the beginning of their bumpy ride and now felt despair. He imagined the Global Community facility as a dark place with some kind of courtyard where they executed prisoners. He shook his head and tried to concentrate.

"Give me the knife and let me try your cuffs," Judd said.

Lionel passed the knife to Judd but lost his grip, and it clattered onto the truck bed. Judd stretched to reach it, the cuffs cutting into his wrists. He had tried twisting his hands, but that only made the pain worse. His hands were swelling, which made it difficult to grip the knife.

"I don't think it's going to work," Lionel said.

"What, you're giving up?"

Lionel grunted. "We've been through a lot of stuff, man. Remember when we were trying to save Nada and her parents and those locusts attacked?"

"Don't do this, Lionel."

"I gave up a long time ago."

When Judd tried rolling over so he could see Lionel, the truck hit a bump. His body flew up a few inches, and he found himself looking at the back of Lionel's head. "What do you mean?"

"Control," Lionel said. "I gave it up a long time ago because somebody else is running this show. We'd have been dead by now if God hadn't taken care of us. And he'll take care of us now, one way or another."

"So you're ready to take the blade?"

Lionel quivered. "I had a dream the other night in Petra. I saw this sharp blade dripping blood and it was mine."

"Why didn't you tell me? We could have postponed the trip."

Lionel chuckled. "The night before that I dreamed I was riding in the pouch of a kangaroo and we were flying over water."

"A kangaroo?"

"Yeah, I could guide him by reaching up and pulling his ears."

"You're strange," Judd said.

"I'm just saying there was no reason for me to tell you the dream when the other ones I've had were so strange."

Judd settled back again and gripped the knife. "You didn't make a dent in these handcuffs."

"I didn't think I would, but I figured we ought to at least try."

Judd looked around the back of the truck bed. A little light was coming through the tiny windows on the sides of the camper. He spotted some rope and small chains at the front. A cardboard box lay on its side with a few rolls of duct tape inside.

"Maybe if you hold the knife on the plastic and I try to twist my arms we can break it," Lionel said.

The road was smoother now, and Judd no longer heard gravel striking the under-side of the truck. He rolled over again, held out the knife, and let Lionel guide it into position.

Lionel grimaced in pain as he jerked the cuffs, trying to snap the plastic. They worked for several minutes without results before Judd felt the truck speed up. The tires whirred and Judd knew they were on asphalt. Albert's muffled curses came from the front, and Judd wondered whom the man was talking to. Something clattered in the front seat, and the truck swerved wildly to the right. Judd rolled onto Lionel and dropped the knife, hoping he hadn't injured Lionel.

Another sound beside them. More tires on pavement. Was there another vehicle?

A high-pitched sound came from the front, and Judd recognized the high-tech weapon. The burst sent a wave of pain through him as he recalled the intense sting of the weapon. Tires screeched beside them, and gravel flew against the side of the truck. Albert sped up, swerving to his left, then to his right, sending Judd and Lionel rolling. Judd tried to hook his foot on something, but Albert swerved again, throwing the two to the other side of the truck bed.

The second vehicle was closing in on them, bumping them from behind and trying to get around. When Judd heard the shotgun blast, he screamed.

＊

Vicki lay on her bed, her face buried in a pillow. She cried so hard she didn't hear Shelly walk in. The girl put a hand on Vicki's back and sat on the edge of the bunk.

"Why did I do it?" Vicki moaned.

"Do what?"

"I was the one who suggested Judd take that flight to South Carolina, remember? If he winds up getting . . . if he gets hurt, it's my fault."

"You know that's not true."

"I told Chloe Williams that Judd was in France and she—"

"I know how it happened, but you can't blame yourself. We have to trust God that—"

"Trust God?!" Vicki screamed. "We trusted God for Bruce, and look what happened to him. We trusted God for Ryan, and he still got trapped during the earthquake. We trusted God for Natalie and Zeke's dad and Chaya. There's a long list we've trusted to God, and they're all dead."

Shelly looked at the floor, and Vicki shoved her face back into the pillow. "He and Lionel are going to die and it's because of me."

Vicki sobbed and Shelly seemed content to sit, not saying anything.

After a few minutes, Vicki sat up and Shelly pulled her close. "You're upset and not thinking straight. You're the one who's said all along that God's in control. He's working his plan, and though we might not understand it—"

"It's too hard! I don't want to be part of

his plan anymore. I don't want to hide or worry about how we're going to eat or if the GC is going to come rushing in on us any moment. Why does God expect so much?"

"Shh," Shelly said, patting Vicki on the back. "God's all we have right now. I've seen you stand up under a lot of pressure, and we're not going to let this stop us from believing that he wants what's best for us."

"Oh, Shelly, I'm so scared." Vicki put her head on Shelly's shoulder and cried. "I can't imagine what's happening to Judd and Lionel right now. I don't want to sleep. I'm afraid I'll have an awful dream about the two of them getting their heads chopped off."

"Listen to me. You know God protected us from the GC with that angel. It's obvious he has more for us to do. Do you think he still has more for Judd and Lionel to do?"

Vicki nodded. "I hope so. It's just that I keep hearing that creepy guy's voice who answered Judd's phone."

"I understand. Right now the best thing we can do is pray. And when you're all prayed out, we'll find something to do. I'll stay with you until we hear from them."

"You will?"

"You bet."

Judd flinched when shotgun pellets slammed against the truck bed and left dents in the metal. The truck immediately dipped to the left, and a horrible scraping made Judd want to plug his ears, but he couldn't. The truck slowed as the smell of hot rubber filled the camper. The tire flopped, ka-thumped, and smoked while Albert tried to keep the truck on the road. He finally veered off, came to a bumpy stop, and called Max on the radio.

The other vehicle screeched to a halt somewhere near the truck. Judd and Lionel tried to see out the small window, but a voice called out to them. "Judd, Lionel, stay down!"

"That wasn't Tom," Lionel said as he and Judd quickly dropped to the floor and lay flat.

A click and a hum sounded from the truck cab. The right front door opened, and Albert plopped to the ground.

"He's coming around the right side!" Judd said.

"Shut up, Judah-ite!" Albert screamed. "I should have taken care of you when I had the chance."

The person at the other vehicle yelled at Albert. "Come around with your hands up and nobody gets hurt."

"It's not me who's about to get hurt."
Albert laughed. A shadow passed the side
window of the truck. Footsteps on the other
side, Tom's. Judd wondered how he had
gotten out of his handcuffs.

"Put down your weapon, Albert," Tom
said.

As soon as Judd heard the weapon fire, he
ducked and pulled his knees to his chest. The
piercing hum jarred him again. There was no
return fire from the shotgun, and Judd
wondered what was happening. "Tom, he's
got the gun set to kill. Don't take any
chances."

Albert screamed again and banged on the
truck's plywood covering. Judd turned and
whispered, "I was hoping he'd give away his
location."

Albert fired his weapon again and someone yelped.

"Ha-ha! I gotcha, you little no-account
Judah—"

Albert's voice cut off midsentence, and
Judd heard a terrific thump. Had Tom been
killed? Why had Albert gone suddenly silent?
Judd was sure the man would turn the gun
on him and Lionel before taking them to the
GC.

The back door opened, and a young man
with sandy hair and rippling muscles looked

inside. "I'm Luke Gowin. You must be Judd and Lionel."

Judd sat up and sighed. "Is Tom—?"

Tom appeared beside his brother. "Right here. I drew old Albert into the open, and Luke did his linebacker routine."

Albert lay on the ground, holding his stomach and panting. Judd felt a strange mix of anger and pity toward the man. A few months ago Judd would have prayed for him and tried to convince him of the truth about God. Now that Albert had the mark of Carpathia, Judd knew his fate was sealed. He felt sorry the man had no chance for heaven, but he was mad at him for trying to harm believers.

"Please don't hurt me anymore," Albert gasped.

Tom limped to retrieve the weapon and threw it in their car, along with another energy clip from the front. After he handed Luke one of the plastic handcuffs, Luke looped the cuffs through Albert's belt, secured Albert's arm behind him, and lifted him into the back of the truck.

Luke's arms were massive and bronzed by the sun. Judd wondered what the boy had done other than play football to be in such good shape. One snip of Luke's pliers and

Judd's hands were free. He rubbed his wrists and raised his hands in the air, trying to get the blood flowing again. Both hands were swollen and had turned a pale blue, but soon they were back to their normal size and color.

"Better get you guys out of here before Max comes," Luke said. He turned to Albert. "We didn't mean to hurt you. And tell your buddy we could have easily killed you today, but that's not our way. We ask you to stop hunting us and leave us alone. If you don't . . . well, God help you."

"I should have set the gun to kill a long time ago," Albert threatened. "Max and I will find you. You're not gettin' away next time."

Luke plastered a piece of duct tape across Albert's mouth and closed the tailgate as Judd and Lionel rushed to the car and jumped in the back.

Luke crawled behind the wheel and told Lionel and Judd what had happened. "Those two guys went after Tom when he and I split up in the woods. I got away, circled back, and hid our car a little farther into the woods. When I saw they had Tom, I knew I had to follow them, but I didn't have a weapon. I raced to one of our supply houses and found the shotgun. When I came back, the truck was gone. I had no idea you guys had been captured too. I went back to the fort and found it empty, so I decided to go looking for those two guys."

"They could have taken me straight to the GC," Tom said.

Luke smiled. "Little brother, it was just a test of your faith in me."

"How did you find their house?" Judd said.

"It took a while. Fortunately I heard the truck when that Max guy took the two dead people to the GC. I backtracked and had just located the house when he got back."

"How did you get Tom out without anyone hearing?" Judd said.

Luke shrugged. "I managed to get through the window and move some of that furniture without making much noise. Tom looked stone cold on the floor, but I had my snippers with me and we got out of there. We were all set to spring on them, but they put you guys in the truck. We decided to take our chances on the road."

"I can't thank you enough for helping us," Judd said. "Did you know they were bounty hunters?"

"We'd heard some rumors from a few people that something was up, but nothing concrete. The GC was always looking for us, but this changes everything. We're going to have to be even more careful."

Luke made his way through a series of back roads, stopping to listen for vehicles passing. They didn't radio ahead to the safe house for fear someone might be listening. When a car passed in the distance, Luke pulled behind a deserted shack, and they got out to wait for nightfall.

"You think Max and Albert will still try to find us?" Lionel said.

"Bet on it," Luke said. "They're in this for the money. And there will probably be more like them roaming the low country for as many people without the mark as they can find."

Judd sat with his back to the shack, his head in his hands. He had been prepared to die, to give his life, and God had used Luke to spare it again. He patted his pockets, forgetting Max had taken his cell phone.

"We can set you up with the latest once we're back at the hideout," Tom said when he found out what Judd was looking for. "You should see all the technical stuff we've gotten from the Co-op."

Lionel smiled at Judd. "Who did you want to call?"

THREE

Vicki's Idea

VICKI and Shelly stayed together the rest of the day talking and praying. They made frequent trips to the main cabin to see if anyone had heard from South Carolina. Sad faces at the computer left Vicki feeling sorry she had come.

"You mentioned we should do something," Vicki said as she and Shelly walked to their cabin. "I think I have an idea."

Vicki led Shelly to a vacant shack and walked inside. The door creaked on its hinges, and dust was piled on the rickety furniture. After Vicki explained her idea, Shelly agreed to help. "We should get Marshall's okay first."

Marshall smiled when Vicki told him their plan. "I have some paint and material you could use for curtains."

The two girls got busy fixing up the cottage. They asked Charlie to help them carry the furniture outside to clean it. By nightfall, the inside was spotless and ready for paint, but Vicki and Shelly were exhausted.

Vicki couldn't stop thinking about Judd, but plunging into a project forced her to keep going, and it felt good to be doing something constructive. She skipped dinner, saying she wasn't hungry, washed up, and retreated to her bunk in the cabin. There she continued writing in her journal.

> *I can't think about Judd dying. The thought is too horrible. I keep hearing that man's voice who answered the phone and it makes me sick. From the time Bruce Barnes started teaching the Bible, I've known that things would get worse. But it always seemed like something far off, an evil in New Babylon. Now the evil has spread so much that we'll have to worry about normal citizens, not just the GC. But a life without Judd . . .*

Vicki put down her pen as someone approached her cabin. Out of breath, Darrion raced inside and fell panting next to Vicki with a cell phone. "It's for you."

Vicki studied Darrion's face for any hint if this was good news or bad, but Darrion quickly rose and ran out the door.

"Hello?"

"Vick, it's Judd."

Vicki covered her mouth with a hand. "Judd . . . you're alive. This isn't your last request or anything, is it?"

Judd laughed and his voice sounded tire* "We just made it to Tom and Luke's place ir South Carolina. You wouldn't believe what happened."

"Tell me. Are you all right?"

"I was until I got shot," Judd said.

Vicki gasped as Judd told her about the weapon the two men had used. "Carl Meninger's looking at it now, but it shoots some kind of laser or heat ray that can kill you. Fortunately it was on stun when he shot me."

Judd went through their flight from Petra, telling Vicki everything about their pilot, Mr. Whalum, how they had made it to the fort in South Carolina only to be chased by two bounty hunters. When Judd described their escape, Vicki felt like she was living it herself.

"Luke was your angel," Vicki said. She told Judd about God's warning and their trip to western Wisconsin. "How's Lionel?"

"Pretty good. We're both scratched up from running through the woods, but I'm looking forward to a shower or a bath and a long sleep. Tom got the worst of it. They think his leg might be infected, so they gave him medicine."

"Any idea when you'll head this way? You're still planning on coming, right?"

"We have to talk about that," Judd said seriously.

Vicki's heart fell. Could Judd have changed his mind? Maybe he didn't feel the same about her. "Go ahead," she said.

Judd took a breath. "We're meeting tomorrow morning to talk about our strategy. It's going to be a tough call whether to stay put or—"

"Judd, get to the part about coming here, okay?"

Judd sighed. "When you're in a situation like we were in, you do some heavy thinking. I thought we were going to die. And every minute I was running I was trying to get back to you. I know God's in control and we're living for him, but a part of me is living to see you again."

Vicki choked back the tears. "Really?"

"I would have paid Mr. Whalum a million dollars to fly us to Wisconsin. And I'm trying not to let those feelings affect our next move, but it's really hard."

"I'm waiting for you," Vicki said. "Just knowing you're all right will keep me going."

She told Judd about Zeke, Marshall Jameson, and the setup in Avery.

"What about the problems you had with Mark?"

"We sort of patched things up before the angel's visit. We haven't really talked since we've been here, but I think he'll be okay as long as I don't do anything stupid."

"You?" Judd chuckled.

Vicki's laughter turned to tears. "Judd, I was so worried about you. I was just writing that I didn't know what I'd do if the GC . . ."

"I know. I feel the same about you. We've come a long way since those first days after the disappearances."

"Do you think it's selfish of us to be so concerned about each other?"

"I don't think it's selfish to really love someone."

Vicki heard someone in the background open a door, and Judd put his hand over the phone. Finally he said, "I need to go. I'll call you tomorrow and we can talk more."

"I can't wait," Vicki said.

※

There were no showers at the plantation, so Judd settled for a lukewarm tub in one of the upstairs bathrooms. The plantation house

was near a slow-moving river miles from any
town. Barbed wire and signs with skulls and
crossbones warned people to keep out of the
contaminated area, and it had worked. A bar-
rier that seemed to be built by the Global
Community blocked the only road to the
house. And with the help of Chang Wong in
New Babylon, planting false information
about the area, Judd hoped to guarantee the
GC would stay away.

The house had fallen into disrepair over
the past fifty years. Banisters that had once
been polished to shine like mirrors were
rotting and in some places lay broken in
pieces. Judd hadn't seen the whole house,
but the kitchen seemed like the most
usable room. Carl had helped Tom and
Luke tap into an electrical wire some
distance away, so no one knew there was
anyone living on the property.

The bathroom floor was so rickety that
Judd wondered if the water-filled tub
might fall through. He gingerly stepped
in and lay back. When the water settled, he
thought about God's mark on his forehead.
That every believer had this mark made it
easy to spot friend or foe, and over the past
few months he had become accustomed
to it. Now, he again saw it as a miracle.
Though Nicolae forced people to take his

mark, God had placed his identifier on people who willingly chose to be forgiven.

He splashed water on his face and watched it drip into the tub. He wondered how he would have acted at the guillotine. Would he have begged for his life? Would he have taken the mark? No, God wouldn't let that happen. Still, Judd wondered where the courage others had shown came from. Was it something God gave the person at the time he or she faced the blade?

While thunder sounded in the distance, Judd dressed and went to the bedroom he and Lionel shared. Together they watched a storm roll in from the coast. Lightning bolts flashed as God put on a light show. Tom had described the wall of water from the meteor that crashed down into the ocean. For some reason, God had wanted this house to stand.

A few minutes after rain began pelting the roof, the ceiling started dripping in a steady stream. Carl Meninger brought in a bucket. "We still have a few holes to plug, so this is our emergency backup system."

From Vicki's e-mails, Judd knew Carl had worked for the Global Community and had helped the kids while they were living in the schoolhouse. He had escaped the GC after

Vicki's final satellite transmission to young people.

"How's Tom doing?" Lionel said.

Carl winced. "His leg's pretty nasty, but we have a lady here who used to be a nurse. He should be fine if he takes care of it."

Carl explained that they had moved from a different hiding place on a small island to this plantation. "What the GC meant for evil, God used for our good. We have lots more room here and it's even safer. Plus, we've learned we have to be more careful about who we trust."

"Not an easy lesson to learn," Lionel said.

※

Judd slept through the night and went downstairs after the group meeting had started. Tom sat in the center of about twenty people with his leg elevated and bandaged. Luke introduced Judd and Lionel to those who hadn't met them the night before. The oldest people were a couple in their fifties Luke had met on an excursion before leaving the island. The couple had become believers after Luke encouraged them to read Tsion Ben-Judah's Web site.

The youngest members were a little younger than Judd. Luke and Tom had found

them on an island not far from Beaufort.
Their ancestors were African slaves, and
though they were glad to be safe, the kids felt
strange living on a plantation.

"You all know the developments and the
new danger we're in," Luke began. He
pulled out a sheet of paper. "This came
from Judd's friend Chang just this morning." Luke handed the message to Carl,
who read the text of Chang's warning
about the new bounty hunter scheme.

"Over the next few days we're going to
figure out our action plan," Luke said when
Carl finished.

"What do you mean?" a girl said.

Carl stood. "There are a number of
things we can do. We can play it safe and
hide, we can concentrate on Internet
outreach and plan small trips—like getting
Judd and Lionel back north—or we can go
on the offensive. Try to beat the GC at their
own game."

"We're looking for as many ideas as you can
come up with," Luke said. "Everybody will be
heard."

Lionel raised a hand. "About Judd and
me, how are we going to get from here to
Wisconsin?"

"That's a good question," Carl said.

"Chang is supposed to send us some more detailed information about the bounty hunters and where they're being used. I'd like to wait until we have that and contact the Co-op before we commit."

Judd nodded. "You've risked your lives for us, and we both appreciate it. We'd be lying if we said we wanted to stay, but we'll wait as long as we need to."

※

Vicki worked at the cottage the next day with a feeling she couldn't describe. Everything seemed lighter. Her heart felt freer, and she hummed as she painted. She had always hated the chores her mother gave her. "When you live in a small space you have to keep things clean," her mother would say.

"Then let's live in a real house like other people," Vicki would say. These conversations usually became heated arguments that wound up getting Vicki grounded. Now she wished her mother could see her efforts.

Maybe Mom can *see me,* Vicki thought. *I wonder what she thinks of Judd. And what does Dad think?*

Vicki imagined a conversation between Judd and her parents. She had always thought of Judd's family as high-class, from a different income level with expensive cars, houses, and friends. But the disappearances had leveled the playing field, both for those left behind and those taken. There was no difference now between Vicki's parents and Judd's. All four were in heaven where even the poorest person on earth was rich.

I wonder if Mom and Dad have actually talked with Judd's parents.

Shelly arrived with more paint and asked Vicki why she was smiling.

"I'd never be able to explain it in a hundred years," Vicki said.

Vicki had asked Maggie Carlson to sew curtains, and the woman had them completed later that evening. Conrad helped secure them over the windows, and Maggie fluffed the corners. "Do you think she'll like them?"

"She'll love it," Vicki said, slipping an arm around the older woman.

The next morning at breakfast, Vicki could barely contain her excitement. Almost everyone in the group knew what Vicki and Shelly were up to, but all had kept the secret. Before the morning meeting, Marshall asked Colin and Becky Dial to accompany him outside. Vicki glanced at Shelly and giggled as they followed.

When Colin and Becky arrived at the cottage, Marshall turned. "One of the qualities of believers who are maturing is self-giving love. People see a need or become aware of another person's pain and they decide to help, not because they are going to get points in heaven or pats on the back, but because they know it's something Jesus would have done."

Colin cocked his head and looked around as others joined the small group. "What's this about?"

Marshall smiled. "You two lost your house and everything in it. For men that's a hard thing, but not the end of the world. A house is a roof and a place to sleep. For wives, it's different. Becky, you lost a home and all the ways you tried to turn those four walls into a place of refuge for your family and friends."

Becky nodded and wiped away a tear.

"We know it's been hard on you, so a couple of younger people suggested we try to make the transition a little easier." Marshall motioned for Vicki and Shelly. "Will you do the honors?"

Vicki stepped forward and opened the door. Though the outside of the cottage had remained the same, the inside had been transformed with the paint, curtains, and cleaning the others had done.

When Becky looked inside, her mouth opened in amazement. She glanced at her husband, who simply smiled and nudged her inside.

"It won't replace your old home," Vicki said, "but we hope you like it."

Becky sat on the bed, put her face in her hands, and wept. She reached out a hand to Vicki and squeezed, then did the same to Shelly.

Then everyone but Colin and Becky moved outside.

Charlie furrowed his brow and squinted at the newly washed window. "Doesn't she like it?"

"More than she can say," Vicki said.

FOUR

Sam's Question

JUDD and Lionel met with Carl and found he had some of the latest gadgets and phones from the Co-op. "Sometimes they deliver supplies, food, and clothes, and other times they have stuff like this." Carl held up a tiny phone about three inches square.

"How do you punch in the numbers on something that small?" Lionel said.

"You don't. It's all voice activated. And look at this." Carl removed a soft plastic piece from the back of the phone and placed it in his ear. "You talk and listen through this without using your hands. You can look at the display to see who's calling, but you never have to hold anything. Some are so small you can actually fix the transmitters to one of your teeth."

Carl handed Judd and Lionel separate

phones and told them to put in the earpieces. "Now watch this. Intercom. Twenty-one. Twenty-two."

Instantly a tone sounded in Judd's ear and Carl's voice came through the tiny speaker. "You can communicate with anyone in the group at a moment's notice from anywhere, as long as they have their earpiece in. With the heightened alert, we're asking everyone to wear these at all times."

"And the intercom works how far?" Lionel said.

"The technology is global, so you could be anywhere in the world and still talk to each other without ever dialing."

"If you can spare some of these, I'd like to take them to Wisconsin with me."

"Just tell me how many you need," Carl said.

The group talked excitedly over meals about their next move. Some took turns at the computer typing out suggestions, while others used pen and paper.

Luke coordinated lookout assignments. One man was a carpenter and had built a small observation tower atop the plantation house accessed through an upstairs room. The land was flat, and anyone could see clearly with the help of high-powered binoculars.

Judd and Lionel took a four-hour shift in

the tower the next afternoon, and Judd used the time to call Vicki. He told her about the group and that their trip north was on hold until they heard from Chang Wong. Vicki said she understood, but Judd could hear the disappointment in her voice.

"There's something I haven't told you," Vicki said. "When the angel Anak warned us to leave Colin Dial's house, he also said something that's been bothering me."

"What did he say?"

Judd heard pages flipping. "I want to get this right. Here it is. Just before he disappeared, he stood right next to me and said, 'You will see your friends again before the glorious appearing of the King of kings and Lord of lords. But one you love will see much pain and will not return whole.' What do you think that means?"

"You think he was talking about me?"

"I don't know. I guess somehow the angel knows about us." Vicki paused. "But I don't know if he meant love in the regular way or the special kind of love . . . I have for you."

"Maybe it's some kind of warning. Or that could have been fulfilled when Tom hurt his leg. If the infection gets worse, there's a chance he could lose it."

"Yeah, it could be, but I had the impression he meant somebody in our original group."

After Judd said good-bye, Lionel put the binoculars down. "What's your gut feeling?"

"I honestly don't know if we should try to move now or wait and—"

"Not about that, about Vicki. What's going to happen with you two?"

Judd looked out the tower window. In the distance he saw the river moving peacefully through the countryside. Large trees dotted the unused fields toward the south. He could imagine a hundred people working them, hot and sweaty, harvesting, planting, tilling the soil. He turned to Lionel. "You know me as well as anybody. What do you think?"

Lionel shook his head. "I'd say you're pretty gone on her, and assuming we can get back, I'm going to have to find some fancy clothes to wear to the wedding."

Judd smiled. "If it happens, would you be willing to be my best man?"

Lionel cackled and stomped his feet. "I was hoping you'd ask."

※

Sam Goldberg put the finishing touches on another edition of his Petra Diaries and read over his words in the computer building.

Sam had included excerpts from the latest message of Dr. Tsion Ben-Judah, who had focused that morning on the words of Jesus. Tsion repeated parables and gave an explanation of each story. Dr. Ben-Judah said he would review the Sermon on the Mount tomorrow.

Sam had begun to notice something strange going on in the crowd as Tsion and Micah spoke. Most people at the site were believers, but every day new people came forward to pray and Sam rejoiced as they received God's forgiveness. Still, hundreds and perhaps thousands were undecided. Another smaller group disagreed with Tsion and Micah and said Jesus was not God.

Sam wrote in his Petra Diaries:

> As Tsion or Micah begin to speak, these defiant ones and those who are not sure about Jesus often fall to the ground as if in pain. They struggle and cry out, tear their clothing, and throw dirt in the air. If you have ever read the story of Jacob when he struggled with the angel of God, this looks exactly like that. They are fighting the very God who has died to save them and calls to them even now.
>
> The Bible talks about this kind of spiritual warfare. I have never seen it so dra-

matic as here in Petra. The people can't walk away from the teaching. It is right in front of them every day, and they cannot escape the voices of truth speaking so clearly.

If you are reading this and you feel this same wrestling in your soul, do not resist God. He loves you and wants to come into your life and forgive you, change you, and make you a new person. Allow him to do that today and end this fight with the God who loved you enough to die for you.

Sam hit the send button and prayed that someone outside Petra would respond to the words. When he opened his eyes, Naomi Tiberius walked into the room. Naomi had become the main computer person at the site, helping train and coordinate communication with Chang Wong in New Babylon. Naomi was a little older than Sam, but he felt attracted to her. Though she had helped Sam become part of her computer team, she hadn't shown much interest outside their work together.

Sam had decided this would be the day he would talk with her about his feelings. He motioned for her and she smiled. A blip on Sam's screen showed he had a new batch of e-mail, but that could wait.

"Do you need help?" Naomi said as she walked up to him.

Do I ever, Sam thought. He glanced at the floor, took a breath, and looked into her eyes. "I have something to ask you that's pretty important."

Naomi sat and stared at the computer. "The monitor looks fine. Is something wrong with one of your programs?"

"No, this is not about computers. It's about us."

"Us?" Naomi said, raising an eyebrow.

"Naomi, I don't know how to say this . . . I've tried not to let my feelings get in the way of our work together, but—"

Naomi put a hand on Sam's shoulder and smiled. "I have sensed that you felt something more than friendship for me." She glanced away, then turned her chair toward him. "I think you're very sweet and kind, and you work very hard at everything you do. You have a heart for God. You're handsome, easy to talk with—"

"Okay," Sam said, sensing bad news, "just get to the point."

Naomi bit her lip. "I don't have the same feelings for you that you have for me."

"Is it my age?"

"Partly perhaps, but—"

"You just said how great I am, handsome, a heart for God. Why can't you like me?"

"I do like you. You're a great friend, and a friend is to be treasured. But friends are always honest with each other. And I would be lying to say my feelings go beyond friendship."

Sam paused. "Do you think you ever . . . you know . . . would your feelings ever change?"

"Again, I must be honest. I don't believe so." Sam looked away, and she grabbed his chair and turned it. "I'm very flattered that you are attracted to me. I'm honored that you've talked to me in such a straightforward way. But you don't want me to lie, do you?"

Sam held up both hands. "It's okay. I won't mention it again."

"Sam—"

"And you don't have to worry about this affecting my work. I'll keep going as long as you need the help."

"Sam, look at me."

Sam sighed and looked at the floor. "I feel like a fool."

"Don't. You're very brave. You were honest with me and you risked getting hurt. I admire that."

"Yeah. I've got a lot of great qualities, but nothing that interests you."

"Sam—"

"It's okay. I understand what you're saying, and I thank you for trying to let me down easy. Now, I have some work to catch up on."

"Sam, don't be upset."

He clenched his teeth. "I'm not."

Sam clicked on his e-mail box and pulled up several messages. Some were in response to recent editions of the Petra Diaries, and others were from kids in the Young Tribulation Force. As Naomi walked away, Sam put his head on the desk. No matter what she said, he still felt awful inside and knew he wouldn't be able to concentrate. He started to turn the computer off when he noticed a message from someone whose last name was Ben-Eliezar.

This is it, Sam thought. *I've been waiting for so long.*

Vicki was elated about Becky Dial's reaction to the spruced-up cottage. The gesture had helped the woman's depression. Vicki had a chance to talk with her a few days later.

"It's not so much the cottage that helped," Becky said, "but to know you guys went to all that trouble and were thinking about me really means a lot."

Judd had called Vicki the day after, just as he had said, but news of his possible return didn't come until a few days later. Vicki took the call in the meeting room and rushed to her cabin to talk.

"I don't know how to say this," Judd said, "but travel right now doesn't look good."

"Is it the bounty hunters?" Vicki said.

"Yeah, I talked with Chang late last night. The GC response to the bounty hunters is positive. The guy in charge of the Rebel Apprehension Program—"

"Kruno Fulcire," Vicki said.

"Right. He's expanding the program throughout the whole United North American States. Chang says that means bounty hunters will be everywhere. Think of it, Vick—with the GC or Morale Monitors, at least you can spot them by their uniforms. Bounty hunters won't be wearing any identifying clothing. And with the kind of money the GC is offering, you can bet these people will target believers and look for as many as they can find."

"Any word on the two who were after you?"

"Chang got into the database and found out they were questioned. They're scouring the countryside for us, so we're on heightened alert. People are keeping watch all day."

"I know what that's like."

Judd paused. "I can't tell you how disappointed I am."

"Me too. But you're safe, and at least we're on the same continent now."

"Part of me wants to forget what the others are saying and just grab a couple of motorcycles and drive up there."

"Sounds exciting but not very safe."

"We also talked about finding a Co-op driver, but with the bounty hunters on the loose, the Co-op will be affected too."

"What was the meeting like? Is everybody in agreement?"

"There are a couple of people who evidently didn't want to risk taking us in. I think they'll be okay, but we have to be sensitive to everybody's feelings."

"So bottom line, you have no idea when—"

"I know exactly when I'll be there, and that's as soon as I can. The very second I get the chance."

🔅

Sam found Mr. Stein speaking with a group of older believers in a cave. When he got the man alone, he showed him a copy of the e-mail from Aron Ben-Eliezar.

"This is one of the sons of the rabbi we helped escape Jerusalem?" Mr. Stein said.

"I'm sure of it. I didn't tell him where I was. He must think I'm in Israel because he asks to see me in Tel Aviv. Read what he says."

> Sam,
> I finally received your note. Thank you for writing. I'm glad to know my parents are safe, but I don't believe they are followers of Ben-Judah. I know they aren't foolish enough to buy what Carpathia says, but they wouldn't turn their backs on our faith.
> Joel and I would like to talk with you, but not by e-mail or phone. And please, don't tell my parents about contacting me. If you can come late tomorrow night, we will wait for you.
>
> Shalom,
> Aron

Aron gave a location and a specific time at the bottom of the page. Mr. Stein folded the paper and took a deep breath. "Something about this troubles me."

"You think they are loyal to the Global Community?"

Mr. Stein shook his head. "No. I think they are lost lambs who need a shepherd, but I don't know what to do."

"Let me go see them. I'll talk with them and tell them the truth."

Mr. Stein pursed his lips.

"The Co-op has pilots. I could ride with one of them."

"Wait here," Mr. Stein said. He climbed down the steep stairway cut into the rock and disappeared.

Sam leaned against the wall and looked out on hundreds of thousands who had made their home in the ancient city. He looked toward the computer building and sighed. *I guess Naomi was kind with what she said, Lord, but it still hurts.*

A few minutes later Mr. Stein returned, his face tight. "I have spoken with the elders about the matter, and they are praying for direction. Unless they disagree with the plan, I will accompany you and we will find Aron and Joel together."

FIVE

Sam's Trip

SAM shook hands with Mac McCullum and boarded the plane that had carried more materials to Petra. The Tribulation Force didn't have to worry about feeding the people here, but there were still ongoing computer and building needs.

Mac talked loudly and didn't hide the fact that he thought it was dangerous to send two believers into Israel. "But if the elders have given their approval, they must have a good reason."

"We all submit to their authority," Mr. Stein said. "If they had told us not to go, there would have been no question."

"Who are you looking for?" Mac said.

"They are sons of a rabbi and his wife who are now in Petra," Mr. Stein said.

Mac asked why the parents weren't going

to talk with them, and Sam explained Aron's e-mail. "We're asking God to help us reach them and bring them out safely."

"Well, I'll be prayin' for you," Mac drawled. "But if those two have resisted the truth this long, I don't hold out much hope for them. How do you know they haven't taken Carpathia's mark?"

"From Aron's e-mail, it sounds like they hate Carpathia like many of the undecided in Petra," Sam said.

"I hope it's not some kind of trap," Mac said.

Mr. Stein asked Mac why he hadn't stayed in Petra, and Mac smiled. "I'd get too fat eating all that manna. Plus, I'm having more fun than a coon in a cornfield flying all over the place with Albie."

"Who's Albie?" Sam said.

"Another Trib Force pilot. I moved in with him after I left the Strong Building in Chicago. We're staying in Al Basrah now, when we aren't flying, which is pretty much all the time. Albie's an expert at trading on the black market." Sam scrunched his eyebrows and Mac said, "You know, getting things without the GC knowing about it and for as little cost as possible. Albie can find just about anything if you can pay the price. That's where this plane came from."

"Do you have phony identification?" Sam said.

"Nah, after what happened in Greece, I know God's looking out for us flyboys. He's got things in control."

Sam watched the Tel Aviv skyline come into view and dialed the number Judd had given him for the man known only as Sabir. Sabir had agreed to pick up Sam and Mr. Stein at an airfield Mac and Albie used. When they landed, Mr. Stein spotted a small car at the end of the runway and Mac slowed the engines. "Should be fine from here. Check with Chang when you want to head back to Petra."

Sam and Mr. Stein thanked Mac and made their way through a chain-link fence that had been cut with wire cutters. Sabir, a short, Middle Eastern man with graying hair and glasses, welcomed them and as they drove told his story of being a former terrorist. Sam hadn't heard about Judd and Lionel's close call with the GC in Jerusalem, and he was thrilled at Sabir's version of the story. Sabir's wife had flown to Petra, and he handed Sam a note to give to her when Sam returned.

As they drove toward Tel Aviv, Sabir gave tips for avoiding the GC. Both Sam and Mr. Stein had hats on and wore long-sleeved shirts so no one could tell they didn't have the mark of Carpathia.

"Why don't you come back to Petra with us after we are through here?" Mr. Stein said as Sabir stopped the car in an alley. "You can take the message to your wife yourself."

"I would like that very much, but so far God hasn't given me peace about leaving. Just the other day I woke up from a sound sleep and felt urged to get in my car. I started it and sat behind the wheel for a good five minutes asking God where I should go.

"I heard no voices, no signs from the sky, so I started driving. A half hour later I was in front of a darkened storefront. I stopped at the curb to get my bearings and saw movement inside. Three people walked out a door and scurried into the night. Something told me I should follow, and I did, with my lights off.

"When they discovered I was there, they began to run. I got out and said, 'In the name of Jesus, stop!' All three stopped dead in their tracks. They turned and walked toward me, and when I turned on my headlights I saw all three had the mark of the believer."

"What were they doing there?" Sam said.

"Hiding. They had not taken the mark of Carpathia and had just become believers a few days earlier. Some people had discovered their hiding place, and they were afraid the GC was coming the next morning. I got them to a safe place before the sun rose."

Mr. Stein patted Sabir's arm. "God has you where he wants you for now, but if you feel in danger, please let us know."

Sabir gave Sam and Mr. Stein final directions and drove away. The sun had set as the two walked through alleys and narrow walkways. A poster caught Sam's eye, and he stopped to examine it. "See the Miraculous Power of Orcus!" The poster gave the date and time, and Sam realized the performance would be that very night.

"I don't like the looks of that," Mr. Stein said, glancing at his watch. "Come on, we only have a few minutes."

Sam was shocked at the difference between the safety he felt in Petra and the evil he sensed in Tel Aviv. The few people they saw in darkened alleys and walkways moved with heads down, fear etched on their faces.

When they reached the meeting place, a public park, Sam and Mr. Stein waited until the correct time and gingerly moved into the open. A block away a stage had been set up with lasers flashing and music blaring. Sam guessed that Aron Ben-Eliezar had picked this place because of the crowds. It would be easier to blend in with thousands than to meet in a private place.

Mr. Stein motioned toward a small fountain, and they sat on a bench, studying the growing mob swarming toward the stage. In the distance, young people whooped and hollered, chanting Carpathia's name and falling in front of a statue suspended above the crowd.

"Aron should be here by now," Sam whispered.

Something beeped to Sam's right, and he noticed a small mound covered by leaves and grass. Sam shoved the debris away and found a walkie-talkie on the ground.

"Okay, pick up the radio and move to your right," a scratchy voice said.

Sam picked up the walkie-talkie and walked toward the street with Mr. Stein. Hundreds made their way toward the stage, and Sam pulled his hat low and tried not to make eye contact with anyone.

"Stop there," the voice said when they reached the edge of the sidewalk. "Look up."

Sam tilted his head and saw a curtain flutter on the third floor of the building in front of them. "Go to the back entrance and take the stairs. Don't let anyone see you come in."

Sam and Mr. Stein followed the directions.

The stairwell had a huge crack in the wall, and plaster was falling onto the steps. When they entered a hallway, a door opened at the other end. Mr. Stein whispered a prayer as they walked toward the open door. Once inside, the door closed and a thin man with a beard stepped forward. He had a bandage on his forehead, but there was no mark of Carpathia on his right hand.

Sam introduced himself and Mr. Stein, and the man stared at them. "I didn't know you were a kid." The man looked at Mr. Stein. "You really know my parents are safe in Petra?"

"Rabbi Ben-Eliezar accompanied us to Masada before going on to Petra," Mr. Stein said. "We have not told them we made contact with you. Are you Aron or Joel?"

"Joel."

"Where is your brother?"

Joel moved to the front window and opened the curtain a few inches. "Don't worry about him. Tell me about my parents."

Mr. Stein told him how he had met the Ben-Eliezars, their concern about their sons, and how they had tried repeatedly to contact them. Joel bit his lip as he listened, his eyes turning to the window.

When Mr. Stein carefully described how they had believed in the message about Jesus,

Joel shook his head. "That is the part I can't accept."

"It is true. It is why we have come all this way at such personal risk. We want to tell you the truth about God."

Joel rolled his eyes. "I have no need to believe in God. There is a scientific explanation for all the questions we have."

"Even with everything that's happened?" Sam said. "The disappearances, the earthquake, the—"

"People believe in God because they've been told to. They have an emotional attachment to their faith because it helps them get through. It helps them deal with their pain. I rely on myself and hard work. If a crisis comes, like an earthquake or another natural disaster, I try harder."

"And what if all your efforts are striving after wind?" Mr. Stein said. "What if you come to the end and find you cannot try harder?"

Joel glared at Mr. Stein. "The only comfort we have in life is to know we have done something worthwhile. We've tried to think independently and struggled to improve the world."

"What happens after you die?" Sam said.

"Nothing. It's over. You get one chance to make a difference and that's it."

"With everything going on in the world,

and with Nicolae executing people without his mark," Mr. Stein said, "does it not make you consider placing your faith in the true God?"

"I have faith in myself that I can improve the world. Outside of that, I have no use for faith."

The door opened and a man who looked slightly younger than Joel came in, breathless. "It's about to start."

Joel introduced his brother, and Aron shook hands with Mr. Stein and Sam. Sam studied his face and hand and didn't see any sign of Carpathia's mark. Mr. Stein repeated the information about his parents, but Joel stopped him. "I want to see how they begin this. Go in the next room."

The window of the shabby apartment faced the stage. Joel grabbed binoculars and watched the introduction of guests as Sam and Mr. Stein went into the bedroom with Aron.

Aron paced as Mr. Stein and Sam sat. "My parents are all right?" he said.

Sam nodded. "Why haven't you answered them?"

"Things have been happening. I came to live with my brother here in Tel Aviv shortly after the Global Community went after those people in the desert. We have tried to exist since then, but my brother, he is not well. . . ."

"Are you open to hearing the truth we have discovered?" Mr. Stein said.

"Perhaps," Aron said. He turned and leaned against the wall. "Ever since Joel took the mark, he has regretted the decision."

Mr. Stein stood. "He took the mark of Carpathia?"

"Yes, though he didn't worship the image."

"Listen to me carefully," Mr. Stein said. "Your soul is at stake. Your brother has made a decision he will regret for eternity. Why haven't you taken the mark?"

"I was hungry. You need it to buy anything. But something seemed wrong about it—not just taking an identification number, but actually identifying yourself with Carpathia."

"You were right not to take it. Now let me tell you why."

Mr. Stein began with an overview of how sin began in the perfect world God had created. The evil one tempted humans, and they chose against God's way. "Throughout the Bible, Satan has opposed God. Now, in these last days, Satan is trying to destroy, just like he has always done. Nicolae Carpathia is the ultimate evil and will stop at nothing to thwart God's plan for good."

"What is that plan?" Aron said.

"To save people from their sins. God sent his own Son to die as a sacrifice for you and me. If we put our trust in Jesus, the Messiah, and ask him to forgive us from our sins, God will do that. Those who were taken in the disappearances, like your sister, Meira, were ones who believed the truth about Jesus. But there is still time to choose—"

"Come and see this," Joel yelled from the next room. "Hurry!"

Sam rushed to the front window and squinted. In the distance a huge monitor showed two men wielding swords that were as long as Sam was tall. The fight seemed staged, but the sound of the steel blades striking each other was real. Finally, one of the men ducked and made a move to his left, avoiding the razor-sharp blade by inches, and struck a blow to the other man's right arm. The crowd gasped as the first man staggered, his severed arm dropping to the stage with a sickening thud.

Blood gushed from the wound, and people near the stage fell back, screaming. The injured man's sword fell, and he slipped to his knees, trying to stop the fatal flow of blood. His opponent held up his sword with both hands and the crowd cheered, encouraging him to finish the injured man.

"It's like watching the Roman gladiators," Sam muttered.

Suddenly a curtain parted, and a man stepped forward. He wore normal-looking clothes, and his hair reached his shoulders. Sam noticed his eyes, which seemed to bore into the man with the severed arm. The longhaired man stooped and picked up the limb from the stage.

The crowd hushed. The hero worship for the winner turned to silence as the man placed the severed arm back in place, grasped it with both hands at the point of the injury, and said, "I have been given power by the potentate. Therefore, under the authority of the risen lord, Nicolae Carpathia, I pronounce this wound healed."

The injured man lifted his once-severed arm and raised a bloody fist above his head. "It's back! He healed my arm!"

Six

Miracle Man

"DID they do that with mirrors?" Sam said, his mouth still open at what he had just seen.

"It has to be a trick," Aron said.

Mr. Stein shook his head. "It is real power, but not the power of God. It is the power of the evil one."

Joel raised an eyebrow. "You mean Bible hocus-pocus?"

"Do not be deceived. You're seeing Scripture come to life. Leon Fortunato calls down fire from heaven by the power of Nicolae. This faker may attempt other miracles tonight to mock God."

The man with the healed arm picked up his sword and raised it in triumph with his new arm. People near the stage fell to their knees and worshiped the miracle worker.

"Do not praise me, for I am only one sent by god," Orcus said as he pointed to the statue of Nicolae. "I am simply his servant. Turn your affection to the one who has the power of life and death and who lives to serve you."

"Praise lord Carpathia!" the healed man said.

"Praise him!" the crowd shouted.

Smoke billowed from the image hovering over the crowd, and everyone lay down before it. Muffled praise rose from the people, and some began singing "Hail Carpathia."

When Orcus raised a hand, everyone quieted. "Your praise has been heard, and I assure you, lord Carpathia appreciates your reverence tonight. And to show you how much he loves you—" he swept his hand forward—"let there be light!"

A great flash of white light bathed the audience. Instead of night, it seemed like day. Sam shielded his eyes and studied the lasers backstage. The light wasn't coming from them but from overhead.

Joel rubbed his forehead so hard that the bandage came off. Sam saw the mark of Carpathia beside scratches and blotched skin. "I've tried to get this off with sandpaper, even tried to cut the skin. But maybe Orcus is right. If he can do these things by the power of Nicolae . . ."

"I need to talk to you now," Mr. Stein whispered to Aron.

Sam followed and Mr. Stein closed the door. "Your father and mother did not want to believe what I told them about God. But after I explained what the Bible says and they heard Dr. Ben-Judah, their eyes were opened. They understood God wanted a relationship with them and that the only way to escape the judgment coming upon this world was to receive the gift of Jesus Christ."

Aron sat and ran a hand through his hair. "I've wanted these past three years to be a bad dream. When you wrote, I thought you were mistaken. My parents could never turn their backs on their Jewish faith—"

"They haven't. Jesus came to fulfill everything the Bible predicted."

With that, Mr. Stein walked Aron through the many prophecies foretelling the coming Messiah. These showed clearly that Jesus had uniquely fulfilled each prophecy and was truly the Son of God. Aron focused on Mr. Stein's words and nodded, asking questions and listening carefully. "If what you're saying is true, my brother has no hope."

"You are right. Once a person voluntarily takes the mark, their eternity is sealed."

"Even if he took it to help me?"

Mr. Stein knelt before Aron. "Don't let your brother's choice affect your destiny. You will not be called to account for his decision. Accept the gift God is offering now."

"Look at this!" Joel shouted from the other room.

Sam ran into the other room with the others and looked out the window. The miracle worker had moved into the crowd and held both swords high above his head. The crowd parted as he walked. "Don't imagine that I have come to bring a sword to divide people. No, like Nicolae, I have come to bring peace."

Instantly, the swords turned into doves, which flew over the crowd. People oohed and ahhed as the birds circled Orcus. "The enemies of our god want us to war and fight with each other. They are like snakes in our midst." The man clapped, and the birds stopped flapping and fell, quickly turning into long, hissing snakes. The miracle worker caught both snakes and held them high so everyone could see. People moved back, some shrieking and fainting.

"There are snakes among us, but our god has helped us identify them. Anyone without the mark of loyalty to the potentate is an enemy of peace. Look around you now and make sure there are no snakes here."

"Over there!" someone screamed. Spotlights swung wildly and stopped on a woman cowering next to a tree. Suddenly, the miracle worker was next to her, both snakes hissing in his hands.

"How did he get over there so fast?" Sam mumbled.

"Are you an enemy of the most high god?" the miracle worker screamed.

The woman trembled and people around her scattered, forming a thirty-foot human ring. Orcus held the snakes higher and asked again if she was an enemy, waving the snakes violently until they became swords again.

"I am Jewish," the woman said, her voice shaking. "I'm not against peace, but I don't want—"

"Silence! I don't care what religion or creed you follow. If you are not willing to show allegiance to Nicolae Carpathia, you are an enemy. Now, will you take his mark?"

The woman fell to her knees and held out her hands, as if in prayer, begging the man. "I can see you are a great man, but please, I cannot show loyalty to a man who kills my people."

With one motion the miracle worker swung both swords and killed the woman where she knelt. The crowd paused, then broke into wild applause, hooting and whistling approval. The man wiped her blood from the blades and turned. "The Jews and Judah-ites are enemies of world peace. They must be identified and eliminated, and you can help. Report anyone without the mark to the Global Community immediately. It doesn't matter if they are strangers, friends, or even close family members. As long as they are living on earth without the mark, they deserve to be cut off!"

The crowd roared, some dancing around the woman's body and spitting. Sam remembered the two witnesses, Eli and Moishe, and how their bodies were treated. He cringed at the cruelty.

"If you know of someone who does not have the mark and do not report them, you are just as guilty," Orcus continued.

"I've seen enough," Aron said, glancing at Mr. Stein. "What do I need to do?"

"Wait," Joel said. "You're not thinking of following these wackos, are you? Didn't you see what just happened? I thought I was wrong, but this proves you need to take Carpathia's mark now."

Aron ignored him and went into the room with Mr. Stein and Sam. When the door was shut, Mr. Stein said, "Becoming a believer in Christ is simple. You recognize that you are a sinner before God. Do you acknowledge that?"

Aron nodded. "I know I've done wrong

things, but I can't see how God can forgive me. Don't I have to do something to make up for it?"

Mr. Stein grabbed a Bible. "In Romans we read this. 'When we were utterly helpless, Christ came at just the right time and died for us sinners. Now, no one is likely to die for a good person, though someone might be willing to die for a person who is especially good. But God showed his great love for us by sending Christ to die for us while we were still sinners. And since we have been made right in God's sight by the blood of Christ, he will certainly save us from God's judgment. For since we were restored to friendship with God by the death of his Son while we were still his enemies, we will certainly be delivered from eternal punishment by his life. So now we can rejoice in our wonderful new relationship with God—all because of what our Lord Jesus Christ has done for us in making us friends of God.' "

"So God becomes our friend simply because we ask him to forgive us?"

Mr. Stein leaned closer. "You could never do anything to wipe away your own sins. We all deserve the judgment of God. But Christ lived a perfect life and took your punishment. Now, if you ask God's forgiveness, he looks at you not just as a person who is going to heaven, but as a person cleansed by Jesus, perfect."

Aron sat and stared ahead. Sam had gone through this same process as Judd and Lionel tried to convince him of the truth. For some the decision was immediate. For others, especially those who were Jewish, it was a more difficult process. There were hurdles they had to overcome that others didn't. Aron had no doubt been raised to believe Christianity was different from Judaism, and for a Jew to embrace Jesus meant that you turned your back on your faith. Sam knew that wasn't true, but would Aron see it?

"So God accepts me just the way I am?" Aron said. "That's almost too hard to believe. I mean, it's too easy."

Mr. Stein smiled. "This is the grace of God. He loved you so much, he sent his Son to die for you. Reach out to him now, Aron."

Aron closed his eyes. "Yes. I need to do this now."

The window in the front room opened and Joel shouted something. Sam opened the door a crack and saw Joel leaning out. "Two Judah-ites! Third floor. I'll keep them here."

Sam closed the door and whispered, "Your brother is telling someone we're here."

Aron shot up from his chair and ran to the

nearest window. Mr. Stein pleaded with him to pray. "It doesn't matter what happens to us here as long as you are washed in the blood of the lamb. Don't put this off."

"I'll do it as soon as we're safe," Aron said. "Come on."

The three climbed out the window onto a fire escape and made their way down. When they were nearly to the street, two uniformed GC Peacekeepers appeared. Sam tried to turn and run, but another Peacekeeper leaned out the upstairs window. They were trapped.

A Peacekeeper led Sam and Mr. Stein to a car, but they took Aron in a separate vehicle. Mr. Stein tried to shout to him what to pray in order to become a believer, but the Peacekeeper struck Mr. Stein with a nightstick and closed the back door.

Sam was terrified as they drove to the GC station. He had heard stories of people who were given the opportunity to receive the mark of Carpathia or have their heads chopped off. He had watched the concert where Z-Van had killed a Christ follower on stage. Now it was his turn.

"I guess this wasn't God's plan for us," Sam said. "We're going to be killed, and Aron won't be able to become a believer."

"Quiet back there," the Peacekeeper said,

rapping on the cage between the front and back seats.

"We must pray for God's help," Mr. Stein whispered. The man leaned close to Sam. In a very soft voice he prayed, "Father, I agree with the psalm David prayed when he was in the wilderness of Judah. 'O God, you are my God; I earnestly search for you. My soul thirsts for you; my whole body longs for you in this parched and weary land where there is no water.'

"Sam and I praise you for your unfailing love, and we will honor you as long as we live. Father, I would lift up my hands to you if they weren't secured behind me, but I praise you now for leading us here and helping us explain the truth to Aron.

"I think how much you have helped me; I sing for joy in the shadow of your protecting wings. I follow close behind you; your strong right hand holds me securely."

Mr. Stein paused and Sam took up the prayer. "Father, help Aron understand the message he's been given and to cry out to you. All those who trust in you will give praise to you, and those who are against you will be silenced."

The Global Community station was in an older section of town, but the building had been renovated and turned into a sparkling

GC facility. The outside was made of stone, and a statue of Nicolae Carpathia towered in front. People were lined up, even at this hour, to take the mark. A few yards from the loyalty application center was the ghastly specter of the guillotine, standing like a soldier at attention.

Sam shivered and leaned close to Mr. Stein. "Will they give us a chance to take the mark, or just take us directly to the guillotine?"

Mr. Stein shrugged. "I was hoping we would be able to have some contact with Aron."

The car stopped in front of the building, and the Peacekeeper got out and went inside the station. The other car with Aron pulled in behind them.

"O God, give us the strength for what we are about to endure," Mr. Stein prayed softly.

Sam's heart pounded in his chest. He couldn't take his eyes away from the guillotine. When the Peacekeeper returned and roughly pulled him from the car, Sam knew he had only minutes and perhaps seconds to live.

SEVEN

Imprisoned!

JUDD'S favorite spot in the plantation house was what Luke called the "Yankee Computer Room" because the house had been used as a hospital for Union soldiers during the Civil War. Many had scrawled their names on walls or into the wood trim, and the owners had left the ancient marks. The room had a comfortable chair and a portable computer, and Judd had fallen asleep several times while writing Vicki.

Though the kids had been separated for quite some time, their Web site had kept going strong. With reports coming in from kids around the world, updates on Dr. Ben-Judah's writings, The Cube, files of information, and Sam's Petra Diaries, there was a wealth of information available to anyone.

But Judd also knew the Global Community was monitoring anything coming from suspected Judah-ites. Tsion Ben-Judah's Web site was a popular destination for GC officials who wanted to see the latest on the "enemy camp." Anything posted on the kids' Web site had to be checked and rechecked to make sure it didn't give out vital information.

Judd loved talking with Vicki, but he also liked writing his thoughts. He had changed a couple of the paragraphs when it seemed they didn't say exactly what he wanted.

Vicki had written about their work on Colin and Becky Dial's cottage. Judd responded:

> I've only known you since the disappearances, but one word I'd use to describe you is giving. You were that way with Ryan Daley, giving him understanding and a big sister to look up to. You've been giving with Charlie. When nobody else wanted to deal with him, you did. I think you're the most giving person I know.

Compliments did not come easy for Judd, but the more he wrote, the easier it was to encourage people. He sent the e-mail and looked through incoming messages. One from Petra caught his attention. He opened it and found it was from Naomi Tiberius. Judd had met Naomi briefly and remembered she was the main computer whiz in Petra.

> *Judd,*
> *I wanted you and the others in the Young Trib Force to know about Sam. He and Mr. Stein have gone to Israel looking for the sons of a rabbi friend. We know from the pilot that they arrived safely in Tel Aviv. Sam was supposed to check in with us after he made contact with the two sons, but we haven't heard anything.*
> *There is a miracle fair going on in the city, so there are many people who would probably like to see Sam, Mr. Stein, and any other believer harmed. Please ask your friends to pray for him and keep praying until we hear something.*

Judd wrote a quick response thanking Naomi for the alert. He checked his unread mail and found an old message from Sam. It explained where Sam was going and that he was trying to make contact with Rabbi Ben-Eliezar's sons. *We are expecting great things and are so glad the elders have approved this trip,* Sam wrote.

Judd couldn't believe he had missed Sam's

message and immediately sent an urgent request to everyone he knew. *Put our friends Sam and Mr. Stein at the top of your prayer list,* he wrote. He explained what he knew and included a portion of Sam's e-mail, leaving out the specifics of the trip in case anyone in the GC might read it. *Ask God to give them protection in a very dangerous situation.*

Judd was curious about the reference Naomi had made to the miracle fair. He found a GC Web site that listed the fairs, and to his surprise discovered they were scheduled around the world in the next few weeks. At hundreds of locations people could watch a self-proclaimed healer do miraculous things. One Web site advertised special coverage and included a button that said, "Watch now!"

Judd clicked the button and was instantly taken to a Web site originating from somewhere in Europe. A crowd had gathered around a stage with a lone man standing at the center. A gallon of blood dipped from the sea was placed beside him on a small table. The man poured some blood into a glass and held it up. "Anyone like a drink? It's fresh."

The thick, red liquid repulsed the crowd, so he poured it back into the container. The camera zoomed in. "By the power given me in the name of the most high Nicolae

Carpathia, I declare this so-called plague to be a fraud."

When the man poured the liquid into a glass, out came clear water. Judd sat up quickly. The fluid in the big container was still bright red. What was poured into the glass was clear.

"Do I have any volunteers now?" the man said.

Several raised their hands. A young woman took a sip from the glass. She smiled, looked at those around her, and said, "It tastes really good." She drained the rest.

The sun shone brightly on the crowd, and the man asked for a bigger container of blood. Like a spotlight, the rays beat down, and people began crying for relief.

"Would you like some refreshment from the sea?" the man said, pointing to the huge red container.

The crowd shouted no, but a worker grabbed the container with a mechanical arm and raised it over them. People screamed, thinking they would be soaked with blood, but when the miracle man tripped a lever, the bottom of the container opened, spilling fresh, cool water on the people.

"I will do even better than that," the man yelled from the stage. He closed his eyes and motioned toward the sky. The sun quickly darkened, and the camera panned overhead. A cloud formed, then spread out and unleashed a gentle rain.

"Bless the name of Nicolae," the man said. "He sends a cooling rain on those who praise him and follow peace." He sneered. "But on those who remain his enemies, on those who refuse his goodwill and insist on their own way, he calls down fire."

A lightning bolt struck, and the crowd squealed. No one seemed hurt, but everyone got the message. "Do not worry. If you are for Nicolae, who can be against you?"

❋

Sam sat in the cell with Mr. Stein, surprised they had been shoved along a corridor to a processing center instead of to the guillotine. The man at the front had asked their names and Sam and Mr. Stein gave them. There was no sense trying to fool the GC about their identities. Neither of them had Nicolae's mark, which was punishable by death.

"Are you Jewish?" the man said.

Mr. Stein nodded. "Both of us."

The Peacekeeper had smirked and shook his head. "Two more for the transport in the morning."

"What do you mean?" Mr. Stein said. "You're sending us—"

The Peacekeeper had backhanded Mr. Stein so hard that Sam thought his friend would fall to the ground. Sam tried to steady him with his body.

"Take them away," the man said to a guard.

"It's okay," Sam whispered when Mr. Stein regained his balance. "Let's go."

The guard had led them to a long line of cells, taken off their cuffs, and shoved them into the last room. Mr. Stein wiped blood from his lip. Sam tried to turn on water from a tiny faucet in the corner, but nothing came out. The toilet in the room smelled hideous.

"What did he mean about the transport?" Sam said.

Mr. Stein shrugged.

A man across the hall slid to the front of his cell. "Are you a Jew?"

"Yes," Sam said.

"They're kicking all of us out of here. They said the guillotine was too good for us, so they're shipping us off to camps."

"Do you know how long you can live without food and water?" another man said from a cell farther away.

"No," Sam said innocently.

"You're about to find out," he said. "They

want to torture us for not taking Carpathia's mark. We're traitors and enemies of the risen potentate. Others get a quick drop of the blade, but we get weeks, maybe months, of starvation and mistreatment."

"I knew this would happen," Mr. Stein whispered, "but I never dreamed I would see it with my own eyes."

The main door opened, and a guard pushed Aron through. Aron fell face-first on the concrete floor. The Peacekeeper jerked him up and threw him into an empty cell at the front and locked the door.

Sam counted seventeen others. A few with the mark of Carpathia who had no doubt broken some law, but most of them were Jews who had not taken the mark. He and Mr. Stein were the only believers.

Mr. Stein called to Aron, but the man didn't move. When Mr. Stein shouted louder, several others told him to be quiet.

"He's either knocked out or dead, so shut up!" a man with Carpathia's mark said.

Mr. Stein and Sam sat on a cot and prayed quietly for Aron.

※

Vicki and the others gathered in the main cabin in Wisconsin and prayed for Sam

Goldberg and Mr. Stein. Though most in the group had never met them, they spoke as if they were close friends.

"Please don't let the GC get to them," Charlie prayed in his simple way. "And if they do, get them out of there. You know they were trying to help others come to know you, so please help them. Amen."

✳

Sam watched for any sign of movement from Aron but saw none. He and Mr. Stein continued to pray, then sang a few choruses, even though some inmates seemed angered by their voices.

Mr. Stein walked to the front of the cell. "Gentlemen, I know not all of you can understand me, but I have been sent here to tell you good news—"

"Why do you think we can't understand you?" a graying old man said. "You're speaking perfect Hebrew."

Mr. Stein turned and winked at Sam. "For those of you without the mark of Carpathia, I say this. On behalf of the true King of kings and Lord of lords, you have a chance to turn from your sin and your rejection of God and begin a relationship with him."

Most of the men turned over on their

bunks, but a few seemed to listen. Mr. Stein was careful not to talk too loud and bring in the guards, but he explained plainly how the men could receive Jesus Christ. When he was finished, Sam noticed Aron moving slightly. Sam called for him and Aron stood.

"If you are ready to pray, do it now before it is too late," Mr. Stein said. "O God, I know that I am a sinner and that I deserve to be punished for my sin. But right now I reach out to you in faith and ask you to take away that sin through the blood of your Son, Jesus. I believe he died on the cross in my place, took my punishment, and rose again three days later, a victor over death. I give my life to you now. Lead me in the paths you desire. Save me from my sin. And I pray all this in the name of Jesus, the Messiah. Amen."

Sam kept his eyes shut tightly as Mr. Stein prayed. He prayed for each of the men and that the guards wouldn't break in during Mr. Stein's prayer. When Mr. Stein finished, Sam looked first at Aron, but the man was again on the floor.

Of the seventeen men, three had the mark of the true believer on their foreheads. Mr. Stein pointed to them, and the three were amazed he could tell they had believed. He explained the mark of God and how everyone who prayed received one.

Finally, Aron stood and Sam was overcome with emotion. The man had the mark of the true believer as well.

"We may not know where they are taking us," Mr. Stein said through tears, "but we know our eternal destination. Our home in heaven has been sealed, and one day we will walk there because of the grace and love of our God."

Mr. Stein asked the three their names and encouraged them with words from the Scriptures. Guards arrived to quiet everyone and turn out the lights.

"Better get some sleep, Jews," one of the Peacekeepers snarled. "You'll be leaving before daylight."

The men grumbled, but Sam settled onto his bunk. Mr. Stein got the attention of one of the guards. "This young man is still a teenager. Tell me you won't have compassion on one so young."

"He's old enough to make his own decisions," the man said. "He didn't take the mark, and he's a Jew. He'll ride with the rest of you."

Sam closed his eyes and thought about Petra. He wished he could be there once more to climb the rock formations and say good-bye to the people he loved. He thought of Naomi. Though she didn't feel the same way he felt for her, she had shown him kindness.

Sam wondered if Judd and the others in the Young Tribulation Force would ever find out what had happened to him. *They will*, Sam thought, *when they get to heaven*.

Sam didn't think he could get to sleep. He imagined the ride to some sickening camp where the GC would put them to work until they dropped. He almost preferred the quick ending of the guillotine to what his mind conjured up.

Later Sam fell into a deep sleep and dreamed of writing a final edition of his Petra Diaries and sending it to everyone in the Young Tribulation Force. In the dream, Dr. Tsion Ben-Judah put Sam's writings on the screen above Petra so everyone could read it.

Sam awakened, smiling. The main door opened and a bright light shone in his face. It was time to leave.

EIGHT

The Reunion

SAM stirred, sitting up on his bunk and watching the guard at the door. The men inside breathed heavily in their sleep and a few snored. Mr. Stein slept soundly, and Sam hated to awaken him.

After the light went out, Sam wondered if the guard was simply checking on them. He glanced at Aron's cell and saw the man was sleeping or unconscious. Sam lay down quietly and waited.

The guard moved slowly past the sleeping prisoners, his footsteps quiet. It was 4:00 A.M. If they were going to be taken before sunup, they would probably be roused in the next hour, but this seemed too early.

Sam listened carefully and was convinced the man had gone, so he settled back on his pillow and sighed deeply. Before he closed his eyes he glanced at his cell door. A man stood there staring at him.

Sam resisted the urge to scream, but his eyes widened and his heart raced furiously. Sam was sure he had never seen this stranger. He wore sandals, a long, flowing robe, had a short beard and piercing eyes. He had no mark, either of the true believer or of Carpathia.

Sam kept his eyes on the man and sat up. "Is it time for us to go?" he whispered.

"Yes." The man's voice was deep, and something about it made Sam want to trust him.

"Are you taking us to the transport?"

The man shook his head.

"Then why are you here?"

"I come in the name of the Lord our God. He is strong and mighty to save. Though the evil one is set on the destruction of the people of God, he will not touch you. There are many praying for you and your friends."

Sam wanted to pinch himself to make sure he wasn't dreaming. He fell out of bed and onto his knees. Tears streaked his cheeks. "I'm not worthy for the Lord to take such an interest in me. Others have died. Why should I be saved?"

Sam felt a hand touch his face, lifting him up. The angel stood next to him, the cell door still closed. "Write these things as an encouragement to those around the world, young one. Tell of the Lord's mighty deeds and give praise to the one who lifts those who are weary of heart."

"You mean my diary—yes, I will." The angel's touch ignited a fire inside Sam, and he couldn't wait to tell Judd and the others. Sam looked at the cell door. They still had to get away from the jail without any guards noticing. And how would they tell Mac about needing a ride without the cell phone?

"Do not let your heart be troubled," the angel said. "Trust in God and the one he has sent to protect you."

Sam nodded weakly. He recalled the story of the apostle Peter being set free by an angel while Peter was chained to two sleeping guards. If God could do that, surely he could help Sam and the others escape.

"Awaken your friend and I will get the others," the angel said. "We must leave quickly."

Sam put a hand on Mr. Stein's shoulder and shook him gently. He opened his eyes and gave Sam a startled look. "Have they come for us?"

"Yes," Sam said, "but not the guards. God has sent someone to rescue us." He pointed at the man who had moved to Aron's cell.

There was a metal clank on the floor as handcuffs fell from his wrists.

Aron rubbed his wrists and stood. The angel spoke from the hall and without moving so much as a finger, the door swung open and Aron stepped outside.

Sam reached for their cell door, and it unlatched as if someone had flipped a switch in another room. Mr. Stein and Sam moved into the hall as the angel awakened the other believers and motioned to them to get up. Sam and Mr. Stein edged as close to the angel as they could as he approached the main door. In spite of the noise of the six inmates walking out of their cells, the others kept snoring.

The main door opened as noiselessly as the cell doors. Sam walked into a holding area, where a guard sat slumped in a chair and another leaned forward on a desk, his hat covering his face. The angel pointed to a shelf above the sleeping guards, and Sam spotted their cell phone in a plastic bag. The angel nodded, and Sam grabbed it.

Each door opened for them as if it were automatic. When they reached the street, they found a sleek minivan parked in front. Sabir got out, smiling, and welcomed the six. Sam turned to thank the angel, but he had vanished like a vapor.

Sam couldn't hold back his praise. "We

thank you, O God, for your protection and your love for us," he said, his arms outstretched toward heaven.

"Come," Mr. Stein said. "We will thank God once we are on our way."

Sabir explained that he had been awakened from a dead sleep and told to come to the GC station. "I got in my little car and a man stood before me, shaking his head. He pointed to this vehicle, and I found the keys in the ignition. If I had brought the small one, we never would have been able to fit all of you in."

"Where are we going?" Mr. Stein said.

"To the airport," Sabir said. "My instructions were very clear. I should accompany you on the flight."

"You're going to see your wife!" Sam said.

"I suppose many prayers will be answered tonight. I said I would stay until God directed me, and now he has."

"Mac needs to know—"

"The angel said everything had been arranged," Sabir said.

As they drove near where the miracle fair had taken place, Aron touched the window and looked out sadly. "What about Joel? Is there no hope?"

"Your brother made a foolish decision,"

Mr. Stein said. "He closed himself to the truth and took the mark of Carp—"

"But I was just as closed," Aron said. "He took the mark partly for me so I could have food."

Mr. Stein turned. "We spoke with your brother before you came in. He seemed upset we had even come. He countered our message at every point."

"He was angry at himself. He knew what you would say about God."

"He turned us in to the authorities," Sam said. "I know you love your brother, and your parents will be saddened by the choice he made, but we can't go back."

Aron nodded. "I understand, and yet my heart breaks for him."

The man buried his head in his hands, and Sam put an arm around him. "My father also made a foolish choice and died before I could speak with him again. I'm so sorry."

Sabir drove to the airfield and parked in the same spot where Sam and Mr. Stein had been picked up the night before. A plane waited on the runway, and they scurried through the fence and quickly boarded. Mac McCullum gave them the thumbs-up sign and had Mr. Stein secure the door.

"When we get in the air, I want to hear all about this," Mac said.

The GC radioed Mac just after takeoff, but he ignored their call. He motioned Sam forward, and Sam sat in the copilot's chair.

When Sam had told him everything, Mac said, "I've seen a lot of strange things in the past few weeks. Bullets going through helicopters, angels blinding the GC, but when I got the call to come get you guys—"

"Someone called you?" Sam said.

"Figure of speech. I was asleep, waiting to hear about my next flight from Chang Wong or Chloe Williams. All of a sudden I was awake and knew I ought to come here. It was as clear as if you'd sent me a fax or called and given specific directions. I just knew."

Sam looked around the cockpit, and Mac asked what he wanted. "Something to take notes with. I need to start a new installment of my Petra Diaries right away."

The reunion in Petra was more than Sam could have hoped for. The four new believers were welcomed warmly as Tsion Ben-Judah announced their arrival at the morning meeting. Several counselors had been trained by Dr. Ben-Judah himself to take new believers and help them learn the basics of the faith. They surrounded the men after Tsion had finished introducing them and whisked them away.

Micah prayed for Jews who were being arrested around the world. "You know, Lord, that these people are being mistreated and killed simply because they have Jewish ancestors. The Global Community considers them traitors, and they are being paraded across international television, humiliated every day. We ask that you would surround these with your love and mercy, and show them the truth that you want them to turn from their sin and accept Jesus Christ as their Savior."

Micah asked the assembly to gather in small clusters. The wonderful sound of voices uniting in prayer echoed off the red rocks.

Sam and Mr. Stein hadn't had a chance to locate Rabbi Ben-Eliezar and his wife, and Aron was anxious to see them. When the groups finished praying, Tsion Ben-Judah introduced Mr. Stein. "This man's own child turned to Christ and he disowned her. After her death, he became a true believer and stands before us today to tell of the mercies of God."

Mr. Stein stepped forward. Sam was proud that he would have a chance to speak to so many. "For those of you who have not yet believed, I plead with you to consider the truth. Christ died for your sins, and he paid the penalty for your disobedience. Do not run from him any longer, but accept his love right now."

A few people near Sam fell to the ground, wrestling with the truth of God. Sam closed his eyes and prayed they might respond while Mr. Stein spoke.

"I would like to ask Rabbi and Mrs. Ben-Eliezar to come forward," Mr. Stein continued. "Are you here?"

From the back of the crowd came a faint cry from Rabbi Ben-Eliezar. He and his wife walked as quickly as they could through the masses. Like the Red Sea, people parted and allowed them to walk through and up a steep walkway that led to Mr. Stein. As they came, he described meeting them and their struggle to believe in Jesus.

Finally, they reached the rocky cliff, and Mr. Stein draped an arm around the rabbi. "They spoke to us of their sons some time ago. When Micah talked about praying for relatives and friends who do not yet believe, my young friend Sam Goldberg took him seriously. He began praying and trying to contact Aron and Joel."

Mr. Stein turned. "Rabbi, Mrs. Ben-Eliezar, behold your son."

Aron stepped out of the shadows of a cave. The rabbi and his wife were so overcome,

Sam thought they were going to topple off the ledge, but they gained their balance and rushed to Aron, hugging him and weeping.

"Their other son was unfortunately caught up in the desire to follow Nicolae Carpathia, but we can rejoice that this one has believed and has returned."

A great roar rose from the crowd as they yelled their praises to God. When the noise died down, Mr. Stein looked at the struggling group near Sam. "What about you? Will you receive the gift of God now?"

NINE

Nicolae's Messiahs

THE DAYS passed quickly for Judd and Lionel in South Carolina. Sam's escape from the GC was all anyone could talk about for a week. Sam's description of the angel and their return to Petra thrilled the group so much that Judd hooked up a video connection with Sam and had him speak to their group.

As time passed, Judd read sketchy reports of bounty hunters discovering more people without the mark. He sent a message to Chang Wong asking for any information on the identity and location of the bounty hunters in South Carolina.

One afternoon Judd was talking to Luke and Tom about their lives before the disappearances. Luke said he had always dreamed of being a shrimper and having his own boat.

"Is that how you got those muscles?" Judd said.

Luke smiled. "I guess. I've always felt like I've been cut out for physical stuff, you know, hard work. I like using my hands, where old Tom here—" he patted his brother's back— "uses his brain, what little he has."

Tom socked Luke in the shoulder. "All brawn and no brain makes Luke a dull boy."

Luke picked a long piece of grass and put it between his teeth. "I've been thinking more about why we've been left here. If those verses about us all being part of a body are right—and it's in the Bible so it has to be— all we need to do is figure out what part we are and do what we were made to do."

"Luke just figured out he's an armpit," Tom snickered. "Smells like one, doesn't he?"

Judd laughed and Luke shook his head. "I'm trying to be serious."

Tom rubbed his face with his hands. "I'm sorry. Go ahead, armp—I mean, Luke."

"I never got to go into the army," Luke continued, "or become one of those special-forces people, but I've grown up around these rivers and marshes and know them like the back of my hand. Instead of sitting here, we could be out there stopping the bounty hunters and finding people who might become believers."

"You gonna do this all over the country?" Tom said. "You read what Chang said. Pretty soon the GC will expand the program, and there'll be more bounty hunters than believers."

"The point is, we can do something now if we want."

"Maybe that's how Lionel and I could get north," Judd said. "We could go along with you."

Luke nodded. "The key is finding the bounty hunter network."

"But what are you going to do once you find them?" Tom said. "Kill them?"

Luke spat the grass onto the ground. "No, that wouldn't be right. But we can sure slow them down, don't you think?"

Vicki gathered with the others in the main cabin to watch the latest from the Global Community News Network. A special Web site had been set up to highlight miracles performed around the world. Many miracle workers looked like average citizens wearing regular clothes, while others dressed in weird outfits. One man tried to imitate the sackcloth Eli and Moishe had worn.

Most of the miracle workers were men, but

there were a few women as well. All claimed they had come under the authority of the risen lord, Nicolae Carpathia, and all had been given power by him.

"Are these demons dressed like people, or are they real people?" Tanya Spivey asked.

Marshall Jameson pursed his lips. "If they're not demons, they're at least humans under the spell of Carpathia."

"I don't like watching this," Charlie said, backing away from the monitor.

Mark pulled up a spreadsheet of information he had documented since the rise of the miracle workers. "The number on the left is how many miracles have been performed. As you go across, you see what types of things they're doing."

"Those are all the same things Jesus did while he was on earth," Darrion said.

"Exactly," Mark said. "They're counterfeiting Christ's miracles just like they have to fake everything else, like the mark on the forehead."

The blood-to-water miracles seemed most popular. One woman had changed water to blood, then changed it to wine. There had been reattached limbs, healing of skin diseases, three blind people given back their sight, and twenty-three lame people made to walk.

The GCNN anchor announced that viewers were in for a treat today because a man in England had asked a miracle worker to heal his sick daughter who lived in Australia. The miracle worker had asked GCNN to set up a live video feed from the man's home, and the network had agreed.

The miracle worker was dressed all in black and stood before a massive image of Nicolae. Five thousand people crammed into the large amphitheater, and crowds spilled out of the venue into the street. Everyone applauded as the miracle worker appeared onstage, accompanied by the father of the sick daughter.

"We are here not to present a sideshow or even entertain you. We have gathered to celebrate the life-giving power of our lord and king." The man knelt before Nicolae's statue. When he stood, he motioned to someone backstage, and workers wheeled a massive monitor into view. The picture rolled and the audio crackled and buzzed.

Conrad shook his head. "If he can heal all those people, you'd think they'd be able to fix the satellite feed."

The miracle worker stared at the monitor, his jaw set, then turned to the crowd. "What you are about to witness has never been attempted before, and it will prove that Nicolae is god and should be worshiped."

"What's he going to do?" Janie said.

"Whatever it is, it's not going to glorify God," Vicki said.

The picture from the satellite feed stopped rolling, and a reporter on the scene in Australia came into view. The woman's face was tight and her eyes red. She stood in front of a simple, ranch-style house with several vehicles parked in the driveway.

"What is the matter, my friend?" the miracle worker said.

The reporter waited through the time delay and said, "Sir, our crew arrived here only a few minutes ago. I went inside to explain what was happening and found those inside watching our coverage."

"So it appears we are a hit with audiences around the world!" The crowd laughed, and the miracle man held up a hand. "Is the young lady still in the house?"

"Yes, but . . ."

The miracle worker raised his lips in a smile. "Go ahead, tell me."

"She is only about sixteen years old. When we got here, a local doctor was with her. Something must have gone wrong . . ." The reporter's chin quivered. She looked at the ground and pulled the microphone away.

"What's happened to my daughter?" the father shouted. "Have they taken her away?"

"Tell him," the miracle worker said, speaking as if he already knew what had happened.

"She is dead. The doctor came out just before we went on with you and told us. It happened a little while ago."

The crowd gasped and the father fell to his knees. He was in such grief that he could only whimper and moan. Finally, he looked up at the miracle worker. "I know you are sent from god, and whatever you ask lord Carpathia, he can do. Please, help my little girl."

The miracle worker closed his eyes and seemed to drink in the man's words. He looked at the audience and shouted, "I tell you the truth. I have not found anyone in the whole of the Global Community with such great faith. In the midst of such distressing news, he looks to the only one who can help."

The miracle man looked at the monitor and told the crew in Australia to pick up their camera and take it inside. When they hesitated, he shouted at them, and the picture wobbled as they hauled the equipment inside.

The living room was filled with people crying and grieving the girl's death. A man with a black satchel and a stethoscope around his neck talked with the woman.

"That is my wife," the father said.

The woman shook a white handkerchief at the camera and moved back. The doctor put out a hand to stop the camera and the reporter, but the miracle man spoke in soothing tones. "Doctor, tell us about the girl's condition."

"This is highly irregular," the doctor said, "I must ask you to leave at once. This family is in the midst of a terrible loss—"

"I know of their loss, and I am here to tell you that you will see victory instead of defeat. Doctor, are you sure the girl no longer lives?"

The doctor suddenly saw himself on television and looked startled. "Yes, of course I am sure. She has no pulse, and she is not breathing. She went into cardiac arrest and died twenty minutes ago."

"What would you say if I could tell you that the mother and father will see this girl alive again?"

"Impossible," the doctor said. "Even if her heart and lungs could begin again, there has been so much damage to the brain that she could no longer—"

"That is enough," the miracle man said. "Take the camera into the girl's room."

"But as I said—"

"Now!" the miracle man shouted.

The camera moved rapidly, family pictures flashing by as the camera raced to the end of a darkened hallway. A door opened and the operator adjusted for the low light.

"Remove the covering," the miracle man said.

The reporter put down her microphone and gently peeled back the white sheet over the body. A thin, dark-haired girl lay on the bed, her face pale and peaceful. The father wept loudly onstage, and the miracle man did nothing to stop him. Suddenly the mother ran into the room, screaming and yelling for everyone to get out.

"Silence!" the miracle man said.

The woman fell back against the bedroom wall. The camera zoomed in on the girl's face. Vicki watched as the miracle man turned and asked the father the girl's name.

"Talitha," the father said.

The miracle man held up both hands and the crowd grew quiet. Kneeling in prayer, the father tried to control his weeping but couldn't. Muffled sobs came from the mother.

Vicki shuddered, guessing what would happen next. The old liar, the one God said from the beginning was a murderer and a

thief, had enlisted this new breed of false
prophets, Nicolae's messiahs.

The miracle man leaned close to his microphone and whispered, "Talitha, wake up."

The words sent a chill down Vicki's spine.
He said it again, this time louder, as if the
corpse couldn't hear. "Talitha, wake up!"

The screen swayed as the cameraman took
a step closer. The girl's eyes fluttered once,
then again. A shriek came from the other side
of the bedroom. The white sheet covering the
girl's body rose slowly as she took a breath.

Thousands gasped in the massive crowd.
The father tried to stand but fell forward
toward the monitor, crying tears of joy. Vicki
and the others in the cabin groaned.

"Talitha, arise!" the miracle man ordered.

The girl's eyes opened fully and she sat up.
In the amphitheater, the crowd went wild—
some screaming, others yelling shouts of
praise to Nicolae. The image of Nicolae
began quaking at the noise and belched fire
and smoke from its mouth. At the home in
Australia, the young girl stood and her
mother embraced her.

The reporter's microphone shook as she
stepped in front of the camera. "If I hadn't
seen it with my own eyes, I'm not sure I
would have believed it. This girl, who had no
pulse, no signs of life for nearly half an hour,

is now walking toward her family. She is alive!"

At this, the crowd raised such a shout that Mark muted the computer speakers. People ran toward the stage, struggling to reach out and touch the miracle man. Cameras switched from the frenzied faces in the crowd, to the weeping father, to the belching image of Nicolae red with fire, to the scene of family members mobbing the young girl in Australia, to the miracle man, smiling, lifting his hands toward the statue, and mouthing the words to "Hail Carpathia."

Vicki and the group sat, stunned at the evil they had witnessed.

Janie broke the silence. "I don't understand. I thought only God could raise the dead."

"The power of evil is real now more than ever," Marshall said. "Tsion has talked about this many times. Satan is being allowed to deceive, kill, and destroy like never before. I don't understand it either, except to say that Satan can only do the things God allows."

Vicki watched the video feed a little longer, then headed back to her cabin with a heavy heart. The last thing she saw was the girl who had been dead kneeling before a statue of Nicolae.

Ten

Chang's Scare

JUDD helped the others put together what Luke called Bounty Hunter Defense kits or BHDs. He noticed some sour looks from the group, and Judd commented later to Lionel about the lack of organization in the South Carolina hideout. At their next meeting, Judd brought up his observations, and the others stiffened.

"Everybody follows Luke and Tom," Judd said. "There's no give-and-take."

"Somebody has to be in charge," Carl Meninger said. "If we voted on everything, we'd never have tried to help you."

Judd nodded. "I think there have to be leaders, no question. But if others just follow, they start feeling left out."

A teenage girl named Shawnda raised a hand. "We came up with our own ideas at the last hideout, and that's when we let somebody in who ratted us out to the GC."

"I can understand being cautious," Judd said. "The goal isn't to make sure everybody has a vote so we rule by majority, but you might be missing out on gifts people have by not including them."

Lionel lifted a hand. "One of the advantages to having this many believers together is the wisdom of numbers. Proverbs says, 'So don't go to war without wise guidance; victory depends on having many counselors.' If we're not working together, we're going to pull apart."

"I wish Tom were here," Luke said, "but he's on watch right now. Let's hear what everybody has to say."

People looked at each other nervously. Finally, Shawnda cleared her throat to speak but was interrupted by two short beeps from the intercom. "We've got movement in the marsh," Tom said. "Somebody's headed this way."

Luke looked at Judd. "Want to take a vote on what we should do?"

※

Chang Wong tried to keep his mind on the tasks at hand but found it difficult. His father was dead, and Chang couldn't shake the thought of the guillotine plunging onto his father's neck. He had dreamed of the man screaming Chang's name just before the beheading. Chang spent the next day erasing any mention of his father's death from GC records. He did not want his boss, Aurelio Figueroa, or anyone else in New Babylon knowing his dad had turned against Nicolae Carpathia at the end.

Chang knew he would see his father again in heaven, and that fact kept him going. But he felt a heaviness, a weight on his shoulders each day he came to work and followed orders.

Chang's sister, Ming Toy, was still in China with their mother, and Chang encouraged Ming to stay there and not risk traveling to the underground hideout in San Diego. Things in China were terrible, but any movement of believers anywhere was extremely dangerous.

Chang spent most of his time outside of work talking and planning with the adult Trib Force, but he had a special interest in the Young Trib Force as well. High on his priority list was helping Judd and Lionel move north to Wisconsin, but with daily reports about new bounty hunters scattered across the South, Chang felt sick. He could see no way Judd and Lionel could leave soon.

Though Chang felt lonely without believers to talk with face-to-face, he prayed almost constantly as he worked at his desk in the palace. The most evil being in the universe was in the same building, but Chang could pour out his heart to God and know that God heard every word, every request, and every praise. Once, Chang had seen Nicolae walking in the courtyard with several GC officials. Chang was praying for the safe evacuation of several Tribulation Force members, and Nicolae had looked directly at him.

Can he read my thoughts? Chang decided to test him. *You are evil in the flesh, the total opposite of the loving God I serve.*

Nicolae looked away and joined another conversation, and Chang was convinced the man couldn't know his thoughts. Only the true God had that kind of power.

As Chang continued his work, accessing data for his boss, he stumbled onto some information from the United North American States. He had been searching for details about the location of bounty hunters. The document before him contained a grid of the southern states with dots. Chang clicked on the dots, and a picture of each bounty hunter popped up with details about where each person lived, their previous occupation, how old they were, if they were married, and other data.

Chang copied the file and decided to wait until he was back in his apartment to send it to Judd. "God, you know what they need to make it back to their friends. I pray this will help them in some way, and if it be your will, help them reach their friends."

Chang opened his eyes and was startled to see a GC Peacekeeper standing beside his desk. "Chang Wong?"

"Yes?"

"You're to come with me immediately."

"Is something wrong?"

"No questions. We're going to Director Akbar's office."

※

Judd was amazed at the way the group flew into action and worked together to make the house look like no one lived there. They had obviously practiced this procedure.

Luke pulled out rickety chairs and a broken table from a pantry. Others raced to the kitchen, gathered dishes and silverware, and hid them upstairs. Carl Meninger took care of the computer equipment and brought the radio with him to the hidden cellar. Within a few minutes the house was transformed into a run-down building.

"We've got two bogeys, both headed toward the house via the main road," Tom said over the radio. "They don't look familiar."

"Take your positions," Luke said.

Everyone ran in different directions, and Judd stared at Luke. "What do you want Lionel and me to do?"

He pointed toward the cellar door, then stopped and cocked his head. "Wait a minute. If these are bounty hunters and they don't turn back at the signs, this might be a good chance to try out our idea. Take one of the BHDs and crawl into the tall grass beside the house. Make sure they don't see you."

Judd and Lionel raced to the supply room, grabbed a kit, hurried out the back, and crawled into the grass. When they were far enough to get a good look at the marsh, they stopped and opened the kit.

"What if it's the guys who caught us, Max and Albert?" Lionel said.

"They'll wish they hadn't come looking for us," Judd said.

A few minutes passed before Tom whispered that a male and female had passed him and were at the warning signs.

"They're coming through the fence. Everybody get ready," Tom whispered.

Judd took out a weird contraption Carl had put together: a curved telescope that allowed the viewer to see around corners or above something taller. Judd fit the pieces together and raised the scope to the top of the grass.

"See anything?" Lionel said.

"Yeah, two coming this way. They're looking at the signs."

"Maybe that'll stop them."

Judd paused, zooming in. "No, they're headed our way."

"All right, looks like we're having company," Luke said into the earpiece. "Tom, follow those guys at a close distance. Judd and Lionel are to the east of the house waiting. We're testing the BHDs."

"You're gonna jump them?" Tom whispered. "What'll you do after that? They'll know somebody's in the house and we'll have to leave."

A long pause. "You're right, little brother. Judd and Lionel, you two keep down out there."

"Got it," Judd said.

Judd and Lionel were far enough away from the house that the two intruders would have to step on them to find them. Judd felt itchy with all the bugs in the weeds, but as the strangers approached, he couldn't move.

"A hundred yards," Luke said. "I'm in the observation tower. Everybody hold your position, except you, Tom, and give me a report if they're coming into the cellar."

Judd put the scope away and waited. Wind

blew the grass above his head. What if the two came around the house and found them? Then what? He took a breath and waited.

※

Chang had been questioned by his boss, Aurelio Figueroa, before, but he had never been in Director Akbar's office. The director's secretary glanced up when he walked in and motioned to a conference room. Chang sank into a leather chair as the Peacekeeper pulled up a questionnaire on a computer screen. Chang saw his picture with the vital statistics such as his age, height, weight, nationality, how long he had been employed by the Global Community, etc.

Has someone found out about my father?

When the Peacekeeper finished taking information, he excused himself, walked out of the room, and closed the door.

Chang realized how isolated he was. If the GC discovered he was the mole, they would have him executed on the spot and the rest of the Trib Force wouldn't know of his death. It might even put the others in danger, since Chang's computer at home carried the contact information for just about everyone.

Chang tried to calm himself. This was exactly what the GC wanted, to upset him enough that he'd appear nervous and say things he didn't want to say. Chang told himself that David Hassid had covered his tracks well and that no one but Chang could access the information in his computer.

By the time Suhail Akbar and the Peace-keeper walked into the room, Chang had stopped sweating.

"I hope we're not keeping you from anything important," Akbar said with a smile.

"What you deem important, Director, is of the greatest importance to me," Chang replied.

Akbar sat. He was in his early forties, from Pakistan, and gave Chang the impression he meant business. He looked over the screen and checked the stats as the Peacekeeper looked on. Chang wondered why two were needed for this meeting, but he quickly put the thought out of his mind.

"I suppose you're wondering why we've called you here," Akbar said, crossing his legs and raising an eyebrow.

"Yes, sir."

"You know we've been searching for an informant inside the palace. A mole."

"Yes, I've been questioned about that already."

"I know, and you passed. But we're putting

all employees through another interview. We know the mole is still here."

"How, sir?"

Akbar clicked on the computer, and a copy of Buck Williams's *The Truth* appeared onscreen. "This, for one. Have you read it?"

"I thought this material was forbidden."

"Good man. It is. But we have to keep tabs on the enemy." He pointed to a section of the first page. "There's information here that no one could possibly know unless he were here in the palace or had a friend inside."

"He tells the truth?"

Akbar frowned. "He gives an accurate account of things that happen here, conversations, activities."

Chang's stomach tightened. If Akbar hooked him up to a lie detector right now and asked if he had ever had contact with Buck Williams, he was sure he would fail. "And you're talking to me because . . . ?"

Akbar smiled and leaned forward. "How well do you know your boss, Mr. Figueroa? How well do you know your fellow employees, like the one who sits in the next cubicle—" he snapped his fingers at the Peacekeeper—"what is her name?"

"Rasha, sir."

"Have you noticed anything unusual about any of these people and how they act?"

Chang's muscles loosened. He could talk all day about his fellow workers. And he would give Akbar as much information as he wanted.

※

Judd lay as still and as low as possible in the grass. Mosquitoes buzzed around his head, and he wanted to swat at them but couldn't.

"I thought they said nobody ever comes to this place," Lionel whispered.

"I guess there's always a first."

The two strangers tromped up the gravel walkway that led to the house. Soon they were on the porch. Judd strained to see their faces, but they were too far away.

"Full alert everyone," Luke said. "They're going inside."

ELEVEN

Intruders

JUDD raised his head and stared at the two on the front porch. One leaned down and looked in the windows, putting his hand to the glass and peering inside. The female knocked and yelled, "Anybody home?" Satisfied, she opened the door.

"No mark of the believer, no uniform, and unarmed," Judd whispered into the intercom. "What should we do, Luke?"

"Everybody hold your positions," Luke said. "Maybe they'll take some food and leave."

Judd heard movement to his left and saw Tom snaking toward the house through the tall grass. He found Judd and Lionel and lay down beside them. "We've never had anybody just walk onto the property like that," Tom said when he caught his breath.

Judd described the two.

Tom nodded. "They could be bounty hunters and we'd never know it until they pulled guns out of their back pockets."

"Shouldn't we jump them before they find someone?" Judd said.

Tom spoke into the intercom. "Luke, we think it might be better to surprise these two rather than the other way around. What do you think?"

"They're in the kitchen," Luke said. "If you can get the jump on them, go ahead."

Tom stood. "Lionel, you stick with me. Judd, go around to the back door and wait for my signal. Let's go."

※

Chang fully answered Director Akbar's questions about his coworkers. He said Aurelio Figueroa was the most loyal employee he had known. The more Chang spoke, the more frustrated Akbar became.

"So you haven't seen anyone in the department who might be funneling information to Buck Williams?"

Only when I look in the mirror, Chang thought. "I know it would make sense for the person to be fluent in computers and technology, sir, but I can't say there's anyone who fits the profile of a Judah-ite near me."

"That's all," Akbar said, waving a hand and clicking on the computer for the next person to interrogate.

Chang went back to his desk, counting the minutes until he could go home and send the information he had gleaned about the bounty hunters to Judd and Lionel.

❋

Judd moved quietly to the back door and waited for Tom's signal. The man and woman rummaged inside. The kids had cleaned out the refrigerator and stored supplies behind a false wall near the pantry, so there wasn't much food left.

"Okay, Judd, now," Tom whispered in Judd's earpiece.

Judd flew inside the door as Lionel and Tom burst into the kitchen. Tom pointed the advanced weapon at the man and woman. They held up their hands and dropped the food, two rancid apples and some moldy bread.

"Hands behind your head, on the floor!" Tom yelled.

Luke ran in and patted them down. "No weapons."

Judd had them hold out their right hands

and saw they had no mark of Carpathia. He helped them up and pulled out two chairs.

The man had a week's worth of beard. He was thin, with dark hair and blue eyes. His forehead was a dark red, sunburned from exposure. The woman also had dark hair and a pretty face. She looked ghostly thin, and her lips were parched.

"You two look like you could use something to eat," Luke said. He motioned to Tom who brought fresh bread and cheese from the pantry and put it on the table.

The two devoured the food in seconds, then drank fresh water. Luke sat beside them and asked where they had come from.

"Savannah," the man said. "We were trying to get to a relative's house in Charleston, but we ran into trouble."

"Bounty hunters?" Tom said.

"I guess," the man said. "They were looking for anyone without the mark. We hid in a shack on the beach, then traveled at night."

"Why didn't you stop when you saw our warning signs?" Luke said.

The woman leaned forward. "We were so hungry and tired, we didn't care. We figured if there was radiation, at least we'd die trying to find food. What is this place?"

"Not so fast," Tom said. "How do we

know you're not working with the bounty hunters or the GC?"

The man shook his head. "I don't know that we can convince you, other than the fact we haven't taken Carpathia's mark."

"Why didn't you?" Lionel said.

"Why didn't *you?*" the man said.

Luke slammed a rickety chair to the floor and it cracked. "We're not the ones asking for food. Now stop jerking us around."

The man held up both hands. "Okay, we've gotten off on the wrong foot." He wiped his hands on his shirt. "I'm Lee McCarty. This is my sister, Brooke."

"And you want us to believe you walked from Savannah with nothing but the clothes on your back and wound up here?" Luke said.

"You don't have to believe anything, but it's the truth. We had enough provisions to make it to Charleston—at least that's what we thought."

"We had to leave our stuff when those guys chased us," Brooke said. "That was a couple of days ago."

Lee pushed back from the table and stood. "Thanks for the food. We're sorry we bothered you."

"We can't let them go back out there," Lionel said, turning to Tom and Luke.

"Sit down," Tom said. "You're the first people we've seen since we found this place, so we're a little skittish. Tell us something about yourselves."

Lee sat and Brooke picked up their story. "Our parents were divorced when we were in high school."

"Names?" Luke said.

"Linda and John."

"Where did you go to school?"

"Milton High in Florida."

Tom wrote down the information as Luke asked who her favorite teacher was and the name of the principal. Brooke answered quickly, and Judd felt sorry for her.

"Look, it's obvious you don't trust us and don't want us here," Lee said. "We'll head north to Charleston tonight—"

"And draw every bounty hunter in the county to us?" Luke said.

"I'd like to hear more about your story," Lionel said. "Keep going."

Brooke nodded. "After the divorce I went to live with Mom and Lee went with Dad. Dad got some kind of religion after the divorce so Mom tried to get Lee back, but that's when the disappearances happened. We all freaked. A lot of our high school was just gone. Dad disappeared, and Mom started drinking. She got killed in the earthquake."

Judd shook his head as Luke drilled Brooke with another question. "What have you been doing since then?"

"We went to live with an uncle and then some friends," Lee said. "We've pretty much just tried to exist."

"I'll ask again. Why didn't you take Carpathia's mark? It would have been a lot easier for you."

Brooke hung her head. Lee glanced at her and sighed. "Dad kept a diary of sorts on his computer. He tried to get me to go with him to church and Bible studies, but I didn't want any part of it. Brooke and I read the journal or whatever he was keeping. He'd been writing out prayers for us, asking God to save our souls and show us the truth."

Brooke looked up. "He said the Lord was coming back for his own and that Satan was going to take control of the earth. My dad wrote that the Antichrist would one day make everyone take a mark and that he hoped his kids would never have to go through that."

"I guess your dad's worst fears came true," Luke said.

"If you've known all that, why didn't you believe like your dad?" Tom said.

"How do you know we haven't?" Brooke said.

"We know," Luke said.

Lee sighed. "I guess if we have to take the mark, we will. We've been avoiding it this whole time—"

"Even though you know they'll kill you if you don't take it?" Luke said.

"We felt like we'd be betraying our dad to take the mark, and we'd betray Mom if we believed what Dad was saying."

"So you're caught in the middle, just like when your mom and dad split up," Lionel said.

"Yeah," Brooke said.

Lionel stayed with Lee and Brooke while Judd and the others went into the next room. Carl Meninger joined them and said he had listened to their conversation through the intercom and had looked up the information Lee and Brooke had given.

"It all checks out," Carl said. "The high school, the teacher she mentioned. Her mom was arrested for drunk driving twice, and there's a Linda McCarty listed among the dead after the earthquake."

Luke scratched his head. "How did they just happen to stumble onto us out here?"

"Maybe it was God leading them," Tom said. "Anyway, all we have to do is explain the truth, and they'll be part of the group."

"You think it'll be that easy?" Luke said.

"There's something else I haven't told you," Carl said, handing Luke a piece of paper. "Chang Wong just sent this. It's a list of the names and locations of every bounty hunter working for the Global Community. With this, Judd and Lionel have a better shot at going north."

Luke nodded. "Okay, but first we explain our beliefs to these two."

"Let Lionel try," Judd said. "I think they kind of connected with him."

"Good. Judd, take him aside and explain. We'll see how they respond. Tom, watch the perimeter from the tower. We're not taking any chances."

Lionel pulled the regular chairs from the storage area and sat at the table next to Lee and Brooke. Brooke asked how Lionel had gotten to the South Carolina hideout and he smiled. "It's a long story."

"We've got time," Lee said.

"Well, I can tell you what happened right after the disappearances." Lionel began there and described what happened to his family. He told them how he had met Judd, Vicki, Ryan, and Pastor Bruce Barnes. "Bruce showed us a video of the former pastor of the church talking about how believers in Christ would one day be taken away or raptured. That's what happened to my family."

"And our dad," Brooke said.

"Right." Lionel explained what the Bible said about God's forgiveness and that a person couldn't work their way to heaven. "God already loves you enough to die for you, and he did that when Christ died on the cross."

Lee nodded. "I get it. If we ask God to forgive us, he will, not because of anything we've done, but because he sacrificed himself."

"Right. It's a good thing you didn't take the mark of Carpathia because that would keep you from becoming a believer."

"Why is that?" Brooke said.

Lionel explained that taking the mark and worshiping Carpathia meant you had chosen once and for all against God. When that decision was made, there was no changing your mind.

As Lionel explained more, he got the feeling that they had already been exposed to the message. They both said it was new to them, except for what their father had written, but they seemed to understand things quickly and didn't ask as many questions as others who had become believers. It almost felt too easy when they asked Lionel if he would pray with them.

"Sure," Lionel said. He closed his eyes and began. Lee and Brooke prayed out loud with him. At one point, Brooke choked up and had to whisper the words. When Lionel finished, he looked at them and they both smiled.

"I feel a lot better, don't you?" Brooke said to her brother.

"Yeah. I'd never have believed just saying a prayer could change things so much. Mom was wrong and Dad was right."

Lionel shook hands with Lee and hugged Brooke. He was about to take them into the next room to tell the others when he noticed something that made his heart drop.

"You guys wait here," Lionel said. "I want to bring Judd and the others in so you can tell them the good news."

"Great!" Brooke said.

Lionel closed the kitchen door behind him and found Judd, Tom, and Luke in the next room talking to Carl.

"How'd it go in there?" Tom said.

Lionel took a breath. "They listened, then prayed. Everything was fine until I looked at their foreheads. They don't have the mark of the believer."

TWELVE

Lionel's Plan

JUDD moved toward the room where Lee and Brooke sat, but Lionel stopped him. "We have to figure out what we're going to say."

"Maybe they didn't understand," Judd suggested. "They might be mixed up."

"They understood," Lionel said. "The way they acted after they prayed seemed calculated."

"But if it's a trap," Judd said, "wouldn't they know about the mark of the believer?"

"Maybe they think that's a hoax and we don't have any mark," Tom said.

"I'll bet you anything they have some kind of transmitter," Lionel said.

"We should take care of them now," Luke whispered.

"What do you mean?" Judd said.

"What I said."

"We can't kill these people. I don't care if they aren't who they say they are. We can't take the chance that they're two innocent—"

"All right. Then we tie them up until we figure out what to do," Luke said.

"We have to go back in soon or they're going to get suspicious," Lionel said.

"Play it like they're part of our family now," Judd said. "We'll keep the others hidden."

"I've got an idea how we can stall whoever they're working with," Lionel said. "Follow my lead."

As the four walked into the room, Lionel beamed and gestured with a hand. "I want you guys to meet our newest members. They're true believers now."

Judd, Luke, and Tom shook hands with Lee. Brooke hugged Judd and said, "I'm so glad we found this place. I can feel the Lord working in my heart already."

"Are there other believers here?" Lee said.

"No, we're the only ones," Luke said quickly.

"But there's something we need to tell you," Lionel said. "A group of believers is supposed to show up in the next couple of days. We've been in contact with them."

"How many?" Lee said.

"A dozen, maybe more. We'll be in touch tonight."

"How do you guys contact each other?" Brooke said.

Judd was sure the two were searching for information, and he was glad Lionel had thought of his plan. The others could get away while the GC or whomever Lee and Brooke were working with got ready to pounce.

"We have a cell phone," Lionel said. "We try to limit our calls to make sure the GC doesn't track us."

"That's smart," Brooke said. "I hate the way the GC operate."

"Me too," Lee said.

"I'll show you around the place," Lionel said. "Let me take you outside first."

Judd, Tom, and Luke quickly met with the others in the cellar while Lionel kept Lee and Brooke occupied. Carl got in touch with Chang Wong in New Babylon with his hastily constructed communications center and asked if there were any GC programs using agents without the mark.

I'm not aware of any, Chang wrote, *but I wouldn't put it past that Kruno Fulcire guy. Let me check it out.*

When Carl asked Chang for a place to escape, Chang suggested talking with Chloe Williams. "She has a better idea of the safe houses and Co-op facilities in your area."

"Vicki can help us," Judd said. "She talked with Chloe a few days ago."

Lionel took Lee and Brooke outside, telling them the history of the property and making up the rest. He could tell they wanted to go inside and explore, but he knew that would lead to more questions and possibly discovering the other believers. "It's time for our teaching," Lionel said, leading them back to the kitchen.

"But we're already believers," Brooke said. "We need to listen to more stuff?"

"Yeah, when you receive God's forgiveness, he puts a hunger in your heart to know more about him. Do you feel that?"

Lee cocked his head. "As a matter of fact, I do have a lot of questions."

Lionel gave them more water and called for Judd. "We're going to have our teaching now. You want to tell the others?"

"Yeah, I'll go get them," Judd said.

Lionel thought of people in one of three camps: believers in God, followers of Carpathia who had no chance of responding to the truth, or people with neither the mark of God nor Carpathia who could still respond. A thought flashed in his mind as he handed Bibles to Lee and Brooke. *If they don't have Carpathia's mark, maybe the truth will get to them. Even if they are Global Community or helping bounty hunters, if God's Word reaches their hearts, they could become believers!*

The thought excited Lionel, and he couldn't wait to go through the material he had chosen. He had them turn to the Gospel of John.

"Why don't you read?" Lionel said.

" 'In the beginning the Word already existed,' " Lee read. " 'He was with God, and he was God. He was in the beginning with God. He created everything there is. Nothing exists that he didn't make. Life itself was in him, and this life gives light to everyone.' "

"Any idea who John is talking about?" Lionel said.

"I don't even know who John is, let alone who this 'he' is who was with God," Brooke said.

"He's talking about Jesus," Lionel said. "The Trinity is made up of God the Father, God the Son, and God the Holy Spirit."

"Why are there three of them?" Brooke said.

Lionel paused and said a brief prayer for them, asking God to take away their blindness.

Judd retreated to a corner of the cellar and called the Wisconsin group. Mark answered and asked how things were going.

"I don't mean to be short, but we've got a situation here and Vicki can help."

Mark handed the phone to Vicki, and Judd quickly explained what had happened. Vicki gave him Chloe's number without question.

"You guys have to get out of there now," Vicki said. "The GC could raid you any minute."

"We feel safe, but we need a destination. I'm thinking, if we head north, Lionel and I might as well keep going until we get to Wisconsin."

"I like that idea." Vicki asked Judd to keep her updated on their plans. "We'll be praying like crazy."

Judd spoke with George Sebastian at the San Diego underground, who passed the phone to Chloe Williams. She seemed upset at first that Judd had called, but when Judd explained their problem, she understood.

Over the past few months, a series of safe houses, homes, and underground shelters had been developed across the country. It was not as sophisticated as Chloe would have liked, but Judd was thrilled they had options.

Judd took information about the groups and ran upstairs. The meeting with Lee and Brooke continued, and by the look on Lionel's face, things weren't going well. Brooke noticed Judd's cell phone and asked if he had heard anything from the other believers.

"I did talk to someone, but we won't know until later tonight when they'll be arriving and how many," Judd said.

The mood was tense throughout the day as the four tried to keep Lee and Brooke occupied. Tom suggested they sleep in an upstairs room he and Luke had cleared out. When they were settled, Judd and the others retreated to the cellar.

Carl Meninger had a video display of the upstairs room onscreen as Lee and Brooke sat on separate beds facing each other. "I wouldn't normally do this, but since we think these two might be—"

"Shh, listen," Luke said, pointing to the screen. Brooke scratched her forehead.

"Don't do that," Lee said. "You'll rub it off."

"I can't help it—it itches!"

"You'll be able to take it off soon, but if these people think we have the mark of Carpathia, we're both dead."

"Can you believe that performance during

the prayer?" Brooke said, taking off her shoe and pulling a tiny object out.

Lionel moved toward the screen. "What's she doing?"

Carl shook his head. "She's calling her boss. That's a phone."

Brooke rattled off a series of numbers. Carl turned up the volume, but they couldn't hear much through the tiny speakers. He put on headphones and relayed what Brooke said.

"She's definitely talking to her boss," Carl said. "She just asked them to hold off on the raid until they get more information about the group coming to the house." Carl pressed the headphone close to his ear and nodded. "Okay, I recognize the protocol they're using. These two are definitely working for the GC."

Judd shivered, thinking how easily the two could have duped them. Carl unplugged the headphones when Brooke moved to the other side of the room.

"They bit on everything we said." Brooke laughed. "The whole thing about our parents, our dad getting religion." She paused. "No, they're pretty primitive as far as technology. We haven't seen any computers at all, so there's no way for them to check our Florida information. I wish they could—it would throw them even further off the track. . . . Yeah, we'll let you know later when the next group is coming in and from which direction. . . . No, sit tight. I think we'll have some good news for Commander Fulcire once this thing is over."

"That's it then," Luke said. "Somehow they've covered up the mark of Carpathia and are leading the GC to us."

"And it makes sense that they couldn't understand what I was saying about God," Lionel said. "They couldn't even pretend to believe."

"But how did they find us?" Tom said.

Judd gave Luke and Tom the information about the safe houses, and Judd and Lionel went upstairs to prepare dinner. When it was time, the six of them gathered around the table, and Judd said a brief prayer. Judd didn't feel right praying for people who didn't exist, so he simply asked God to bless the food and protect their friends. Brooke and Lee said an enthusiastic, "Amen."

Everyone went outside after the meal, giving the kids in the cellar enough time to move their things to an outside shed. They would wear the clothes on their backs and take as much computer equipment and tools as possible in backpacks. Moving on foot wasn't going to be easy, but Carl had found someone who could give them a ride to the next safe house.

"God sure was good to lead us here," Lee said. "I can't believe we're actually going to get to see our dad again."

"I look forward to seeing my family again too," Lionel said. "Almost as much as I want to see old Nicolae finally fall."

"How's that supposed to happen?" Brooke said cheerily, though Judd detected an edge to the question.

"The Bible says Nicolae is going to fight God with his armies but that he'll be captured, along with his false prophet. They'll both be thrown into a lake of fire, and the army will be wiped out."

"Wow," Brooke said. "Nicolae seems so powerful. You think that can actually happen?"

"I *know* it will," Lionel said. "I've read the end of the book."

At the selected time, the cell phone rang and Tom answered. He walked a few paces into the front yard and spoke softly. Judd knew the call was from the cellar, and Brooke and Lee strained to hear what Tom said. As Tom walked back to the group, Judd noticed Brooke touch her shoe.

"There's twenty of them," Tom said when

he returned. "They're at a safe house south of us."

"Twenty?" Lee said.

"We've got room," Tom said, "but they can't get here until late tomorrow night. Some kind of car problem."

"That'll give us more time to fix up the place," Brooke said.

"Good thinking," Luke said, motioning for Brooke and Lee to follow. "Let me take you guys down to the river. You know, God's love is like a mighty river. There's a ton of verses that talk about that. . . ."

Judd, Lionel, and Tom quickly ran to the house and helped the others with the last of their things. There were tearful good-byes to Tom. Carl gave him a big hug and said they would wait for him at the Barnwell, Georgia, safe house.

"Hopefully we'll meet tomorrow night after we get things settled with these two," Tom said.

"I've left a few surprises for the GC downstairs," Carl said. "Don't go poking around down there. And you'll be without any kind of computer connection."

"It's okay," Tom said. "We'll catch up tomorrow night."

After dark that night, Judd sat up with Lee

and Brooke, talking about the ways God had changed his life. Judd didn't hold back explaining exactly what God had done, thinking it might have some effect, even on people with Carpathia's mark.

Tom came in a few minutes before midnight and gave Judd a nod. The others had escaped without being noticed. Judd couldn't wait until it was his turn to leave, but he knew they had to come up with a good plan to keep Lee and Brooke occupied.

One more night and we'll be on the move north, Judd thought.

THIRTEEN

Out for Blood

EARLY the next morning Judd took the call from Carl Meninger letting them know the group was safe in a hideout at Barnwell, Georgia. Carl and the others had walked miles through the low country until they had reached a major roadway running north and south. There, they hooked up with a fearless Co-op member who had risked his life and his truck to help the kids escape.

"I've e-mailed Chang from here, and he says the GC have called in the big guns for tonight's raid," Carl said. "There's a group north of Charleston who want to help transport you. The pickup will be at the same place as ours, but they'll take you to a different location to be safe."

Judd noticed Lee and Brooke listening near the door. "Okay, then we'll expect you guys late tonight. Can't wait to roll out the red carpet. We're fixing up some rooms so you'll feel welcome."

"I couldn't help overhearing," Brooke said when Judd hung up. "The new members are definitely coming?"

"Yeah, and I talked with Luke about setting up watch for them. They'll be coming from the south, so we'll need some lookouts to welcome them and make sure we don't get any unfriendlies."

"What do you mean?"

"Global Community."

"You don't think they know about this place, do you?"

Judd took a breath. "The GC know a lot about everything. They could be following our people, or bounty hunters could be out there. We need people on all points of the perimeter." Judd handed Brooke a radio. "We'll use these to communicate."

"Lee and I will be honored to help."

Throughout the day, Luke and Tom coordinated the meeting place with believers in Walterboro, South Carolina. The two mapped out their trail as Judd, Lionel, Lee, and Brooke worked on upstairs rooms.

"Some of these are clean," Lee said. "Were there people staying here before?"

"We haven't been here long," Lionel said.

"From what I've heard, a lot of people have moved through here in the past couple of years."

Judd broke away from the others and went to the cellar to call Vicki. He remembered Carl's reminder and noticed wires running along the foundation and several weird contraptions under the staircase.

Vicki was glad to hear from Judd and said she felt good about their escape plan. "We've been praying for you guys nonstop."

Judd told her that he would try to e-mail or call as soon as they arrived at their location, but not to worry. "Lionel and I have been kicking around an idea for after we get out of here."

"What's that?"

"It's clear that coming up there is going to be risky right now if we try to fly in or even drive. The GC is cracking down on anybody without the mark."

"Then you need to stay there until it's safe," Vicki said.

"Not necessarily. We've mapped out a list of safe houses nearby that Chloe Williams gave us. We'll need more as we go north, but what if we get enough supplies together and hoof it to Wisconsin?"

"You're not serious."

"Totally. There's no way the GC can patrol the forests, what's left of them, and if we can make it to different safe houses every few days for rations and maybe grab some rides with Co-op members, it could happen. I don't know how long it would take, but at least we'd be moving in your direction."

"Judd, you know how much I want you back here, but this sounds . . ." Vicki giggled.

"What?" Judd said.

"I was just thinking about a story I read about a guy . . ." Vicki paused. "No, I don't want to say it."

"Come on, tell me."

"Well, he wanted to show his girlfriend how much he loved her, so he started out in California and walked all the way to his girl-friend's house in Pennsylvania and proposed to her."

Judd smiled. "Sounds pretty devoted."

"I wasn't saying that to make you . . . you know, to plant some kind of idea or anything . . . oh no, I've really done it this time."

Judd chuckled. "That story obviously didn't happen during the Tribulation."

"Right, that just popped into my head. I'm sorry."

There were footsteps above so Judd lowered his voice. "Listen, there are a lot of miles between us right now, but I'm going to make it back. When I do, we're going to be a great team again."

"Be careful, Judd."

❋

Vicki hung up with Judd and wished she could do something to help him. Her days at the Wisconsin hideout were good, with plenty of work and new opportunities for reaching out through the Internet. The kids' Web site had been listed as forbidden by the Global Community, but that only made people want to read it more. It was like the list of "banned books" Vicki remembered at her local library. The controversy made more people want to read them, though she didn't understand how you could check out a "banned" book.

The Global Community had developed a program that infected The Cube, the kids' high-tech presentation of the gospel, but Jim Dekker, who had created the program, quickly discovered how to defeat the virus. With the rise of the miracle workers around the world, many undecided wrote with questions, and Vicki found many believers who were confused. They couldn't understand how these false messiahs could do the same types of miracles that first-century Christians had witnessed.

Vicki spent most of her time answering e-mails, helping with the mundane cleanup and cooking, or fixing up run-down cabins. Charlie was a big help moving heavy things and finding new lumber. Phoenix spent most of his waking hours following Charlie around and never let the young man out of his sight.

Other than Judd, the person who weighed most heavily on her mind was Cheryl Tifanne. Cheryl had become a believer shortly after being rescued from a GC holding facility in Iowa, and the girl was pregnant. She wasn't due for another few months, but Vicki wondered if the girl would be strong enough to deliver the baby.

Cheryl had asked Josey and Tom Fogarty to be the parents of the child after he or she was born, but Cheryl was having second thoughts. As the baby began to move in Cheryl's womb, it became more real and Cheryl wondered if she had made a mistake promising the child to someone else.

"If I hadn't become a believer, I would have probably had an abortion," Cheryl said. "Now I can see that every life is precious, even though the baby's father abandoned me."

"You'll probably stay right here with the

Fogartys," Vicki said. "You'll help raise the child."

"But it's going to be hard just handing the baby over," Cheryl said.

"From what I know about pregnancies, your emotions are going to go all over the place. It's important to keep asking one question: what's best for the baby? If you keep that in front at all times, you won't be swayed by how you feel. You'll do the best for the child."

Cheryl nodded. "It's not going to be easy, though. I can't imagine holding the little thing in my arms and then giving it away."

Vicki put an arm around the girl. "God will show you what to do when the time's right. And he'll give you the strength to do something good."

Cheryl caught her breath. "Did you feel that? He kicked! Right here. Feel."

Vicki put a hand on Cheryl's stomach and felt something pressing against her. A bump appeared on Cheryl's skin and Vicki giggled.

"I think that's an elbow. Can you believe it, Vicki? A brand-new life coming into the world and at a time like this." Cheryl trembled as the baby moved again. "I'm scared for the little thing. How are we ever going to take care of it?"

Vicki didn't answer. She knew there were

no guarantees for any of them. The GC could find out about their camp and wipe it out in a few minutes if they wanted. But for some reason God had left them here, scared and outnumbered, for a reason.

Judd tried to stay calm throughout the day as he and Lionel led another study of Scripture. Lee and Brooke tried to act interested, but Judd could tell the Bible annoyed them. Judd scooted close and asked Brooke to read a few verses. As she staggered through the words, Judd looked closely at her forehead. Whoever had covered their marks had done a good job. All of Brooke's scratching had left a crease in the makeup, and Judd thought he saw air bubbles under the rubber-like covering.

Tom and Luke gathered the radios and a few BHDs, put them in backpacks, and hid them in the woods to the north of the house. When the six gathered for dinner, Tom gave Judd a discreet thumbs-up.

"Why don't you lead us in a prayer tonight, Brooke?" Luke said.

"Oh, I-I-I couldn't, really."

"Nonsense. I know you're new and all, but you've got to get over being nervous about praying in public. Give it a shot."

"Yeah, go ahead," Lee said with a smile.

"Okay." She folded her hands and closed her eyes.

Judd felt a twinge of guilt listening to the girl stammer. He wanted to punch Luke for suggesting it. All they needed was for her to slip and pray something to lord Carpathia and the whole Global Community would come down on them. When Brooke finished with, "I pray to Jesus, amen," Judd heaved a sigh of relief.

Two hours later, Luke handed Brooke and Lee a radio and asked them to follow. He placed Tom at a spot near the river, then left Lionel a few hundred yards to the south in a marshy area.

"We'll leave you two together by the fence there," Luke said. "You'll have the best view if anybody comes up the road."

"Let's hope it's your friends, the believers," Lee said.

"Exactly," Luke said. "Judd and I will walk west toward that field. That'll give us a better view of the air in case the GC decides to join us."

"Got it," Lee said.

Judd and Luke jogged west through the tall grass. A faint orange glow shimmered on the horizon as the last of the sun played through the trees.

"How far do the radios reach?" Judd whispered when they hit the tree line and headed north.

"Two, maybe three miles. Far enough that when we get out of range, there won't be anything those two can do about it."

Judd hustled after Luke. They had left Tom near the river because of his bad leg. He was closest to the meeting point.

Judd stopped when he heard a creaking sound. "Is that a helicopter?"

Luke shook his head. "It's just cicadas. Come on."

Tom checked in on the radio and the others answered. Luke had been careful to place everyone out of sight of Lee and Brooke.

"Nothing here," Lee said into the radio.

"Check," Luke said. He turned to Judd. "I'll bet a hundred Nicks they've called their GC comrades. You could see the gleam in their eyes when we dropped them off. They're out for blood."

"It's sad, really," Judd whispered.

"What do you mean?"

"You know the GC had to brainwash them. Who knows what would have happened if Nicolae's goons hadn't gotten to them."

Judd's mind played back the scene in Israel where he had injured a Morale Monitor. Judd had never heard whether the boy had lived or died, but he knew they were in a war. Nicolae Carpathia would stop at nothing to wipe out his enemies, and Judd was in that group.

"All right, we're in place," Luke said when they had run to the back of the property. "Everybody check in."

"Everything's quiet over here," Tom said.

"Same here," Lionel said.

Luke stared at the radio, waiting for Brooke or Lee. Finally, Brooke's voice cut through the static. "Nothing over here. Luke, where did you and Judd go? We lost sight of you."

"See that little copse of trees on the knoll? We're about a hundred yards farther to the west."

"Wave to us."

"Something's not right," Judd whispered.

Luke nodded and keyed the microphone. "I don't want to give our position away. What's wrong?"

"It's just that we can't see any of you, and we don't want to get separated. You know, in case the GC come," Brooke said.

"I should have thought of this," Luke muttered. He keyed the mike again. "Okay, how about I come back to you and Lee goes with Judd?"

"Are you crazy?" Judd whispered.

"That's good," Brooke said. "I'll head toward you now."

"What are you doing?" Judd said. "You can't switch places—"

"You head toward the meeting place, and I'll stall these two," Luke said to Judd.

"How?"

"I don't know, I'll think of—"

"Hold your positions, guys," Lionel said over the radio. "I see movement. Brooke, Lee, do you see something moving this way from the road?"

"No, there's nothing . . . wait. Yes. Now I see it."

Two clicks sounded on the radio, the secret signal for everyone to run. Luke took off into the brush and Judd followed, his heart racing. The soft light of the sunset had given way to a creeping darkness, and Judd found himself at Luke's heels, dodging trees and crashing through the underbrush. Had Lionel's report about movement been true or a ruse to keep Luke away from Lee and Brooke? Had the GC moved in to arrest the small band of the Young Tribulation Force?

Judd gasped for breath as they plunged deeper into the woods. He hoped they would find Lionel and Tom at their meeting place.

FOURTEEN

Race to Walterboro

JUDD ran as fast as he could through the thick brush. They passed a swampy area, and Judd made sure he followed Luke's exact steps. He hoped Lionel would catch up with Tom, who knew the area well.

Brooke's voice cut through the songs of crickets and grasshoppers. "We think that's a deer moving on the road. Luke, are you on your way?"

Luke stopped and tried to still his breathing. Judd bent double, his hands on his knees.

"I'll just come over there and you meet me," Brooke said.

"Negative," Luke said. "I thought I saw headlights coming this way. It could be our people."

The radio was silent for a few moments,

and then Brooke's excited voice came again. "Okay, tell us if you see anything else."

"Maintain radio silence until I give the word," Luke said, then clicked the radio twice.

Luke started running again at an even pace. Judd was beginning to think their plan would work. When they reached the clearing, Judd helped Luke pull out the hidden backpacks, and they both put one on. Luke knelt, his eyes darting back and forth at the scene. The moonlight cast an eerie glow through the trees.

"Where are they?" Judd whispered.

Luke put a finger to his lips. "Somebody's coming."

Tom crashed through the brush and fell into the clearing. He held his injured leg and gasped for breath. "Didn't think I was going to make it."

"Where's Lionel?" Judd said.

"Didn't see him. I thought he'd catch up with me before I got here."

Tom reached for a backpack, but Luke waved him off. "You don't need the extra weight on that leg. I'll carry it."

"You don't think he's back there waiting, do you?" Judd said.

Luke stood, concentrating on the sounds around them. "I hear something."

The three squatted and Luke grabbed a large stick. Luke's muscles tensed as he got a firm grip. Footsteps sloshed through water behind them, and then Lionel ran in from the west and plopped down in the middle of the group. "I went too far," he gasped. "Tried to find Tom . . . then got turned around . . . sorry."

"It's okay," Luke whispered, pulling out a compass.

"Did you really see something on the road?" Judd said.

Lionel pulled his backpack on, shifted its weight forward, and shook his head. "Thought you guys could use some help. Brooke was about to come your way."

Luke pointed northeast. "Tom sticks with me and you two bring up the rear. We're headed two miles in that direction, then—"

Tom held up a hand and glanced into the brush.

"What is it?" Luke said.

"I don't know, I thought I—"

The brush crashed around them as Lee and Brooke hurtled into the clearing. Judd's first thought was to run, but when he saw Brooke reach into her boot, he knew he had to stop her. He lunged, but Brooke stepped back, avoiding him, and Lee's sharp kick to Judd's stomach crushed air from his lungs.

Before Brooke could push the button on

the phone, Luke threw the extra backpack and knocked the phone into the brush.

Brooke fell back. "You Judah-ites are dead!"

"So you're not real believers after all," Tom said. "What a surprise."

"All four of you on the ground. Now!" Lee yelled.

"You're forgetting something, GC boy," Luke drawled. "There's four of us and two of you." He grabbed Lee by a wrist, turned his arm behind him, and the man went down hard. Brooke screamed, and Judd clamped a hand over her mouth.

"Hand me some duct tape, Tom," Luke said.

Luke taped their mouths, hands, and feet. Lionel found the phone and gave it to Luke, who dropped it on a rock and smashed it with one stomp.

"How many are coming for us?" Luke said, ripping the tape from Lee's mouth. "And no yelling."

"I'm not telling you anything."

Luke knelt beside Lee. "I know a big snake pit not far from here. You two should feel right at home."

Brooke's eyes widened, and she shook her head violently.

"I don't know how many exactly," Lee

said. "Enough to flank the road and capture
as many Judah-ites as you said were coming."

Luke glanced at Tom. "That changes
things. Get on the phone to our people and
tell them to hold their position. We'll head
to the—" Luke stopped, then pulled Tom to
the side, whispering something in his ear.
Tom nodded and walked several yards away
and held the phone to his ear.

"You're not going to get away," Lee said.
"If we don't get you, the bounty hunters
will."

"Maybe you're right," Luke said. "Maybe
we'll get caught. But when your Global
Community crumbles, remember we told
you what would happen. You're on the
losing side."

Truck brakes squealed in the distance. Lee
started to call out, but Luke slapped the tape
back on his mouth.

Judd looked back as they headed east
toward the river. Lee and Brooke lay squirm-
ing on the ground like earthworms. Judd had
caught his breath from Lee's kick, but his heart
pounded like a jackhammer. The GC were at
the house and would be searching for them.

After they had run a hundred yards east,
Luke pointed left and they switched directions. A few minutes later, he held up a

hand. "I'm hoping they think we're headed for the river and that we're trying to meet our group downstream. They shouldn't find Lee and Brooke for a while, so it should give us some time. You guys ready?"

Everyone nodded and followed Luke. A series of explosions erupted, and Judd wondered if the GC was destroying the house or if the blasts were Carl Meninger's work. The four slogged through a marsh and onto dry ground. With Global Community troops nearby and bounty hunters ahead of them, Judd smiled. He was finally going home.

❋

Vicki stayed up the entire night with Shelly, Janie, Darrion, and Tanya. The five prayed for Judd and the others, asking God to protect them and the rest of the southern Young Tribulation Force. Vicki was amazed at how quickly the time passed as they prayed, read passages out loud, and talked. Cheryl tried to join them but couldn't stay awake.

Marshall Jameson had given Vicki an old road atlas he had found, and Vicki turned to the South Carolina page. She held the map as they prayed, wondering if Judd and Lionel were on any of the small roads she saw.

The angel's words came back to her. Was it

possible that something would happen to Judd on the way? Vicki prayed silently, not wanting the others to know her fears.

At 5:30 A.M., after hours of prayer, the phone rang and Vicki beat the others to it. "Hello?" she said.

"It's Judd. We made it."

Vicki fell to her knees, tears welling in her eyes. The others crowded around and tried to listen, hugging each other and thanking God.

"We made it to Walterboro about fifteen minutes ago," Judd said. "You won't believe where we're holed up. It's an old Baptist church the GC thinks is condemned. There's a basement with an underground hideout."

Vicki ran a finger over the wrinkled map in her hand and found Walterboro. She flipped back to the main page and tried to judge the distance between Wisconsin and South Carolina. It was such a long way. When she could speak, Vicki said, "How's Lionel?"

"Good. We're both tired and scratched up. I'll write and tell you all about it."

Vicki hung up and thanked everyone for staying up with her, then went to her bunk. She thanked God again for keeping Judd and Lionel safe and fell asleep asking him to bring them back soon.

Over the next few days, Judd and Lionel planned their trip north, contacting Chloe Williams about the different safe houses along the way. Judd found out that Carl Meninger had indeed set explosives inside the plantation house to destroy materials left behind.

"They weren't meant to hurt anybody, but I'm not going to cry if GC soldiers lost their lives."

Judd furrowed his brow. "We're not here to kill people. The GC will label us terrorists if we start—"

"Look," Luke said, "we're in a battle. You don't think there are casualties in war? They're chopping off the heads of believers every day."

"But why stoop to their level?" Judd said.

Luke stared at Judd. "If we'd have taken care of those two back at the house, we'd probably still be there."

"Right. Kill all the GC we can," Judd said, throwing his arms in the air.

One of the Walterboro believers came in to quiet them, but they still argued.

"Tom and I are going out tonight on a little mission," Luke said. "We could use the help."

Lionel shook his head. "If you're going to do something violent, we can't support you. We'll pray for you and ask God to protect you, but we don't see this as the answer."

"Fine," Luke said. "Just remember who rescued your nervous hides."

Judd checked with Chang Wong, who said there were three reported injuries at the plantation house but no troops killed. Chang said he felt more and more isolated in New Babylon and longed to escape.

For the next three nights, Luke and Tom slipped into the darkness with supplies and blackened faces. News came over GCNN of fires deliberately set in South Carolina. All were said to be the homes of bounty hunters.

"Maybe they'll get the message and stop what they're doing," Luke said.

But a week later, Luke and Tom failed to return from a night mission. Everyone assumed they had gone to Barnwell to join their other friends, but no one was sure. Judd and Lionel made final preparations to leave, though they didn't want to until they found out about Luke and Tom.

The next afternoon, the Global Community made a startling announcement. The Walterboro group surrounded the television in their dark underground as Commander Kruno Fulcire held a press conference.

"I will allow questions, but before that I have an important message and directive for all citizens of the Global Community," Fulcire said. "We have conducted a pilot program, a test for the entire world. I'm pleased to say that our bounty hunters have had great success in ferreting out our enemies. There have been hundreds of people in the southern region of the UNAS delivered to GC headquarters.

"We want to thank those who have participated, some at great personal cost and peril. I have communication from the highest levels who say they appreciate your efforts."

Fulcire looked at his notes. "However, with recent terrorist actions taken against GC forces and especially targeting bounty hunters, we have an alternate plan we hope will be instituted not only in the southern region, but in all the United North American States, and eventually, throughout the entire Global Community."

Fulcire held up a shaded map of the southern region. "I have authority from the very top to issue this proclamation. If you are listening to my voice and you are in this shaded area and still have not complied with taking the loyalty mark to our risen lord, you have forty-eight hours to receive that mark.

"After the forty-eight-hour period, we will observe a zero tolerance policy and institute a vigilante law. This means any loyal citizen with a valid mark may kill an unmarked resident on sight. There is no longer any excuse to have neglected your duty. You must come forward at once.

"Citizens who exercise their rights and eliminate lawbreakers will be rewarded. Simply bring the body to the nearest GC facility for processing."

Judd couldn't believe what he was hearing. They had escaped the GC and bounty hunters, and now ordinary citizens would be their enemies. People in the room clucked their tongues and tsk tsked.

"Sir, what happens if a citizen mistakenly kills a person with a valid mark?" a reporter said after Fulcire finished his remarks.

"The murder of a loyal Carpathianite is punishable by death," Fulcire said. "Anyone, no matter what the intentions, must be sure the person they accuse of being an enemy does not have the mark here or here." He pointed to his forehead and right hand. "I suggest caution, but if you know someone is a Judah-ite or simply doesn't have the sense to take the mark, your action will be rewarded."

"Is there a preferable way to execute enemies of the Global Community?" a female reporter said.

Fulcire smiled. "A dead traitor is a dead traitor. The weapon is up to the loyal citizen. Personally I would like to see these people suffer, but that is up to the vigilante."

The crowd of reporters laughed, and Lionel turned to Judd. "What does this do to our plans about heading north?"

"If we're ever going to leave, now is the time," Judd said.

FIFTEEN

Heading North

JUDD and Lionel crammed supplies into backpacks, and one of the Walterboro group gave them a solar cell phone. They had mapped out a series of safe houses and campsites through South Carolina, North Carolina, Virginia, Kentucky, Indiana, Illinois, and finally Wisconsin. Judd checked with Chloe Williams to find Co-op flights or trucks headed in that direction, but Chloe confirmed Chang Wong's fears. Some Co-op drivers had been caught, while others had cut down their routes and had trouble just getting supplies to needy groups.

Judd had not only mapped out their travels but also tried to estimate the time for each leg of the trip. On some days, if someone gave them a ride, they could travel as much as fifty miles. Other days, when they were hiking through mountains, they could go five or ten miles at most. They planned to hike through the night and hide during the day, either at a safe house or somewhere in the woods.

The Walterboro group gathered round them after dark, put their hands on Judd and Lionel, and prayed for their safety. Though they hadn't stayed long, Judd felt like they were part of his family. They had risked their lives, and Judd was emotional as the believers huddled around them.

One of the members had agreed to drive them from Walterboro to Barnwell, where the members of Luke and Tom's group stayed. The man had disabled the car's brake lights and they set out after midnight, driving by moonlight. When they saw headlights of an oncoming car, they pulled over and hid until it passed.

Carl Meninger met them in the wee hours of the morning and showed Judd and Lionel where they would sleep, but both agreed to stay up the rest of the night and sleep during the day. Carl took them to the makeshift computer room, and Judd and Lionel spent a few hours writing e-mails and finding out more about the Global Community's latest actions.

Judd became so engrossed that he didn't

notice Carl walk into the room, tears in his eyes. "What's wrong?" Judd said.

"We just saw a report about the bounty hunters," Carl said. "Tom and Luke are dead."

The news hit Judd like a punch in the stomach. He staggered from the computer to the TV in the next room.

"More now on the deaths of two young men thought to be the arsonists terrorizing South Carolina," the reporter said. The picture switched to grainy video shot the night before and three bounty hunters standing by two bodies.

"This is them, all right," one man said. "We caught them with gasoline they used to start the fires last night."

The camera moved closer, showing the faces of Judd's friends. The two brothers who had saved Judd's life lay lifeless on a wooden pallet. Someone had tried to rub the shoe polish from their faces, but the Global Community spokesman said their identities weren't important. "What is important," the man said, "is that a message is sent to our enemies. As you can see, neither of these two had the mark of loyalty, so the bounty hunters will receive their reward, as will any citizen who finds and exposes anyone not bearing lord Carpathia's mark."

Judd went back to the computer and sat, numb from the news. After a brief memorial service for Luke and Tom, Judd wrote Vicki: *I can't help thinking they wasted their lives trying to stop the bounty hunters. They could have done so much more for the cause. I don't want that to happen to us.*

※

Over the next few weeks, Vicki waited for Judd's calls each morning and kept track of his progress with the atlas and a pen. Judd would give his location, and Vicki drew lines from South Carolina, through North Carolina, and into Virginia. Vicki had a celebration when Judd crossed into a new state.

Judd and Lionel were taking great care in their travels, but Vicki couldn't help but worry when they'd report seeing a GC squad car or even a normal citizen. Their job, as Judd told it, was to walk or ride as far as they could each night, taking as few chances as possible. If they had the choice to go ten miles over a mountain with no chance of seeing anyone, or going five through a more populated stretch, they went over the mountain.

"The thing that scares us most is dogs," Judd said one morning. "The ones that have survived all the plagues seem meaner, and they bark their heads off at anybody on foot."

The next day, Vicki didn't get a call from Judd until late in the afternoon. She worried throughout the day until the phone rang.

"We found a cave just before sunup," Judd said from a Kentucky cave, "but since this place is so remote, we decided to find the safe house. It was set back on a hill overlooking a little town, but when we got there, several GC officers surrounded the place."

"Those poor people," Vicki said.

"The GC stormed it and came out with nothing."

"You think the people were tipped off?"

"I hope so. Anyway, we won't be able to get the ride we thought we would."

"I don't like how long this is taking," Vicki said.

"We're being safe," Judd said.

Vicki tried to keep her mind on other things, like working on the kids' Web site. The best activity she found was cleaning and fixing up run-down cabins. The physical work helped keep her mind busy. She, Charlie, and the others completed the cleaning or construction of a new cabin about every two weeks.

Every few days, Marshall Jameson would get a call for Zeke from some secret believer who had heard about what the man could do to people's appearances. Zeke had set up shop in one of the renovated cabins and thrived on helping people. With the coming of Carpathia's mark, there was only so much Zeke could do, but everyone who visited him went away happy.

In her weak moments, Vicki counted the cost of not flying to meet Judd in France. They would be together now if she had, but she wouldn't be available to Cheryl.

Cheryl had reached the halfway point of her pregnancy but didn't seem to gain much weight. She tried to eat healthy but felt sick to her stomach most of the time. She slept late each morning and could remain up only a few hours before going back to bed. Marshall, who had some medical training, admitted they needed to find someone to help with the baby's delivery.

Mark searched the Web for any information. Josey and Tom Fogarty were so concerned that Tom offered to drive to find a doctor, but they couldn't locate one. Vicki sat with Cheryl and tried to calm her. Several times the girl was afraid she had lost the baby, and then it started to move again and Cheryl sighed with relief.

"Zeke can do just about everything else— you think he could help?" Cheryl said.

Vicki smiled. "You're lucky you have so many people who care about you. We're going to find some help." But deep inside, Vicki wondered if they would or if the job would be Marshall's.

❋

After the event with the Global Community in Kentucky, Judd and Lionel covered even less ground each day and camped about every other night. They both grew dirty, unable to take showers for days at a time, and let their beards grow. Lionel said Judd looked like a mountain man, while Judd said Lionel looked like a fuzzy cartoon character.

"Which one?" Lionel said.

Judd just laughed and waved a hand. They had become closer since hearing of the deaths of Luke and Tom. Judd felt more comfortable talking with Lionel about Vicki, and Lionel shared some of his fears about the final years of the Great Tribulation.

"We're playing for keeps now," Lionel said. "It's like everybody in the world is hunting us, and all we're trying to do is survive."

"Everybody in the world needs what we have," Judd said, "but if they've taken Carpathia's mark, they won't be able to believe."

Judd had never traveled through this part of the country, except by interstate, and he was surprised at how beautiful the land was. Even with the earthquake and the fires that had consumed grass and trees, he could still see the beauty of God's creation.

When they reached the Ohio River and prepared to cross, they decided against using bridges for fear they'd be spotted, so they found a small boat and pushed across. The river was swifter than Judd anticipated, and they drifted a mile downstream.

Three days of hard traveling through rugged terrain left them on the outskirts of Salem, Indiana. They found the safe house in the wee hours of the morning and called from nearby. A groggy-voiced man answered and hurried to open the door of an old farm-equipment store.

The man, Eustice Honaker, pulled them inside and put a finger to his lips. He led them through the building to a secret compartment under the stairs. The room was belowground, only about five feet high, and housed nearly a dozen people sleeping on cots.

Eustice pulled Judd and Lionel to the corner and whispered, trying not to awaken anyone, "There was a boat stolen a few nights ago along the river."

"That was us," Judd said.

Eustice pushed a tattered baseball cap back and scratched a bald spot. "The GC has scoured the countryside for you two. Somebody spotted you from a bridge, I guess."

"We didn't see anybody in the woods while we traveled," Lionel said.

"They're out there, and they've enlisted everybody in this half of the state to find you. I thought you'd been caught."

What was supposed to be an overnight stay turned into weeks as Eustice and the others convinced Judd and Lionel that to leave would be suicide for both them and the local group. If Judd had felt isolated before, he now felt so cooped up he could scream. There was no Internet connection, so he got his news about other believers from Vicki and those he talked with via phone. Vicki read him huge chunks of Buck Williams's *The Truth,* and Judd relayed the words to his new friends.

Since there was no sunlight inside the hideout, Judd snuck out before sunup and put the phone in some weeds where he knew it would recharge, then retrieved it late the next night. The only news about local happenings came from a local radio station.

After moving several hundred miles and feeling the freedom of being their own bosses, Judd and Lionel felt like their future was in someone else's hands. Several times the group had given the okay for them to leave, only to have the Global Community strike up another round of raids. The weeks turned to a month, then two. Finally, five months since leaving Israel, Judd and Lionel began the final leg of their journey.

Eustice and the others gathered around and prayed, as so many of the groups had done. They also prayed for the Wisconsin believers and Cheryl's baby in particular.

As Judd slipped into the muggy Indiana night, he knew he was closer than ever to reconnecting with his friends.

"You ready for this?" Lionel said.

Judd nodded. "I've never been so ready."

※

Vicki raced to the main cabin for Marshall Jameson. Cheryl Tifanne had been complaining of pain in her stomach for hours, and everyone hoped it would go away. She still had several weeks to go before giving birth, but Vicki could tell from the girl's sweating and increased pain that something terrible was happening.

Marshall had tracked down a midwife who was a believer and through a coded e-mail had discovered she lived about two hours away. Marshall sent a message, grabbed his coat, and headed for his vehicle. Mark followed him out the door.

Vicki glanced at the clock. If it took Marshall two hours to get there and two hours to get back, it would be 4:00 A.M. before he returned.

When Cheryl screamed, Vicki rushed inside the cabin.

Shelly held the girl's hand, placing a cold cloth on her forehead. "She's not getting any better, and her stomach's getting tighter."

"Just hang on, Cheryl," Vicki said. "Help is on the way."

※

Judd took the lead and headed up a rocky slope in the moonlight. "How does it feel?" he said to Lionel.

"Nothing against those people, but I was about to go crazy."

They had been walking two hours, Judd making sure they were headed north. A cool breeze blew out of the west. "I don't care if we spend the rest of the trip outside. The fresh air is like a taste of heaven."

Just after midnight they came to a ridge that Judd thought must have been created by the wrath of the Lamb earthquake. On the left of the hill was a swiftly moving stream, and to the right was a rock face that heaved up.

"Your call," Judd said. "You want to go around?"

"Nah, let's go over the top. I'm ready for some adventure."

The climb up the slope wasn't difficult. There were some loose stones, but the grade was about as steep as a ski slope Judd had climbed as a kid. But when they reached the top, Judd's mouth gaped. The other side was a sheer drop.

"You sure you don't want to go around?" Judd said.

Lionel looked at his watch. "We'll save time this way. Come on."

Lionel led the way. Judd was glad there were only a few clouds out or they wouldn't have been able to see the footholds. About halfway down, Lionel held up a hand and told Judd to wait. "Let me get closer to the bottom before you climb down."

Judd sat back against a boulder, and a cascade of tiny rocks skittered down the hill. Lionel shielded his face with a hand and scowled.

"Sorry," Judd said in a loud whisper.

The passing clouds looked like a train, spreading out across the black sky. Judd wondered if Vicki was still up. He thought about calling her but decided against it.

Lionel moved slowly, so Judd got another foothold and stepped onto the boulder so he could relax. As he put his weight on the huge rock, he felt something move. Another cascade of tiny rocks plunged down the incline, and then the boulder itself tipped forward.

"Hey, look out!" Judd yelled, jumping from the rock and sliding down a jagged slope.

The boulder moved like a turtle, slow and easy as it tilted. Then, as the ground shifted and the earth beneath it gave way, the rock gained momentum and crashed down the hillside.

Judd grabbed a bush growing straight out of the hill and hung on. He glanced down, seeing Lionel frantically trying to move out of the way. Judd screamed as the rock bounced left, heading straight for Lionel.

ABOUT THE AUTHORS

Jerry B. Jenkins (www.jerryjenkins.com) is the writer of the Left Behind series. He owns the Jerry B. Jenkins Christian Writers Guild, an organization dedicated to mentoring aspiring authors. Former vice president for publishing for the Moody Bible Institute of Chicago, he also served many years as editor of *Moody* magazine and is now Moody's writer-at-large.

His writing has appeared in publications as varied as *Reader's Digest*, *Parade*, *Guideposts*, in-flight magazines, and dozens of other periodicals. Jenkins's biographies include books with Billy Graham, Hank Aaron, Bill Gaither, Luis Palau, Walter Payton, Orel Hershiser, and Nolan Ryan, among many others. His books appear regularly on the *New York Times*, *USA Today*, *Wall Street Journal*, and *Publishers Weekly* bestseller lists.

Jerry is also the writer of the nationally syndicated sports story comic strip *Gil Thorp*, distributed to newspapers across the United States by Tribune Media Services.

Jerry and his wife, Dianna, live in Colorado and have three grown sons.

Dr. Tim LaHaye (www.timlahaye.com), who conceived the idea of fictionalizing an account of the Rapture and the Tribulation, is a noted author, minister, and nationally recognized speaker on Bible prophecy. He is the founder of both Tim LaHaye Ministries and The PreTrib Research Center. He also recently cofounded the Tim LaHaye School of Prophecy at Liberty University. Presently Dr. LaHaye speaks at many of the major Bible prophecy conferences in the U.S. and Canada, where his current prophecy books are very popular.

Dr. LaHaye holds a doctor of ministry degree from Western Theological Seminary and a doctor of literature degree from Liberty University. For twenty-five years he pastored one of the nation's outstanding churches in San Diego, which grew to three locations. It was during that time that he founded two accredited Christian high schools, a Christian school system of ten schools, and Christian Heritage College.

Dr. LaHaye has written over forty books that have been published in more than thirty languages. He has written books on a wide variety of subjects, such as family life, temperaments, and Bible prophecy. His current fiction works, the Left Behind series, written with Jerry B. Jenkins, continue to appear on the bestseller lists of the Christian Booksellers Association, *Publishers Weekly*, *Wall Street Journal*, *USA Today*, and the *New York Times*.

He is the father of four grown children and grandfather of nine. Snow skiing, waterskiing, motorcycling, golfing, vacationing with family, and jogging are among his leisure activities.

Hooked on the exciting
Left Behind: The Kids series?
Then you'll love the dramatic audios!

Listen as the characters come to life in this theatrical
audio that makes the saga of those left behind
even more exciting.

High-tech sound effects, original music,
and professional actors will have you
on the edge of your seat.

Experience the heart-stopping action and
suspense of the end times for yourself!

The Future Is Clear

Check out the exciting Left Behind: The Kids series

BOOKS #37 AND #38 COMING SOON!

Discover the latest about the Left Behind series and complete line of products a

www.leftbehind.com